At the Mountains of Madness

A Classic Lovecraftian Sci-Fi Horror Adventure –
Ancient Mysteries and Cosmic Horrors

A Modern Translation

Adapted for the Contemporary Reader

H. P. Lovecraft

Translated by Tim Zengerink

Table of Contents

Preface - Message to the Reader

What If You Could Help Rebuild the Greatest Library in Human History?

Thousands of years ago, the Library of Alexandria stood as the crown jewel of human achievement — a sanctuary where the collected wisdom of every known civilization was gathered, preserved, and shared freely.

And then, it was lost.

Through fire, conquest, and the slow erosion of time, humanity lost not just books — but ideas, dreams, discoveries, and stories that could have changed the world forever.

Today, the Library of Alexandria lives again — and you are invited to be a part of its restoration.

Our mission is simple yet profound:

To rebuild the greatest library the world has ever known, and to translate all timeless works into every language and dialect, so that no seeker of knowledge is ever left behind again.

By joining our movement to rebuild the modern Library of Alexandria, you become part of an unprecedented mission:

- **Unlimited Access to the Greatest Audiobooks & eBooks Ever Written:**

  Instantly explore thousands of legendary works—Plato, Shakespeare, Jane Austen, Leo Tolstoy, and countless more. All instantly available to read or listen, placing a complete literary universe at your fingertips.

- **Beautiful Paperback & Deluxe Editions at Printing Cost**

  Own any title as an elegant paperback, deluxe hardcover, or stunning collectible boxset—offered to you at true printing cost, delivered straight to your door. Build your personal Library of Alexandria, crafted for beauty, built for durability, and worthy of proud display.

- **Fresh Translations for Modern Readers—in Every Language & Dialect**

  Enjoy timeless masterpieces reimagined in clear, contemporary language—no more outdated phrases or obscure references. Alongside the original versions, we're tirelessly translating these classics into every language and dialect imaginable, ensuring accessibility and understanding across cultures and generations.

- **Join a Global Renaissance of Literature & Knowledge**

  You directly support expanding our library, publishing deluxe editions at true cost, translating works into all global languages, and bringing humanity's greatest stories to people everywhere. By joining today, you're not just preserving a legacy of masterpieces; you set in motion a powerful wave of literary accessibility.

Become a Torchbearer of Knowledge.

Join us for free now at **LibraryofAlexandria.com**

Together, we will ensure that the light of human wisdom never fades again.

With gratitude and a shared love of knowledge,

The Modern Library of Alexandria Team

Visit:

www.libraryofalexandria.com

Or scan the code below:

Introduction

The Apex of Cosmic Horror: Science, Discovery, and the Terror of Truth

H.P. Lovecraft's At the Mountains of Madness, first written in 1931 but initially rejected and only published in 1936 by Astounding Stories, stands as perhaps the most ambitious and expansive tale in Lovecraft's canon. In it, we find the culmination of his philosophical and literary vision—a chilling blend of science fiction, horror, and speculative history that redefines the boundaries of human knowledge and dares to imagine what lies beyond them. This novella is not merely a tale of monsters or haunted places; it is a carefully constructed revelation about the origin of life on Earth and the horrifying insignificance of humankind in the vast, cold architecture of the universe.

Framed as a firsthand report by Dr. William Dyer, a geologist from Miskatonic University, the story details a disastrous scientific expedition to Antarctica that uncovered not only the ruins of a prehuman civilization but the fossilized—and soon reanimated—remains of its creators. What begins as a routine scientific endeavor transforms into an existential nightmare as the team encounters the ancient city of the Elder Things, beings who arrived on Earth before life as we know it even existed. Dyer's urgent purpose in recounting the expedition is not scientific acclaim but warning—he hopes to dissuade any future expeditions from probing too deeply into the planet's forgotten past.

The structure of At the Mountains of Madness mirrors the intellectual descent of its protagonist. It begins in the familiar world of science, logic, and academic rigor. Lovecraft's opening pages are filled with geological terminology, historical references, and the measured tone of an academic report.

But as the explorers push deeper into the Antarctic wasteland, that rational framework begins to crack. They uncover hieroglyphs, architectural anomalies, and artifacts that challenge the very foundations of biology, archaeology, and evolutionary theory. And then, of course, they awaken what should have remained buried.

This trajectory—from rationalism into madness—is Lovecraft's central motif. The horror lies not in what is seen, but in what is understood. The ancient city in Antarctica is not haunted by ghosts or demons. It is a monument to knowledge too vast, too old, and too alien to coexist with the human mind.

The great irony is that these monstrous discoveries come not from superstition but from science—from the pursuit of understanding. At the Mountains of Madness is not an anti-science story. It is, rather, a warning about the limits of human perception and the price of unfiltered truth.

Ancient Civilizations and the Fragile Human Mind

Lovecraft's mythos reaches its most elaborate form in this novella. Here, the reader encounters the Elder Things—bioengineered, starfish-shaped beings who descended from the stars, created life on Earth, built colossal cities, and warred with other cosmic entities like the Great Race of Yith and the monstrous Shoggoths. These beings are not demonic—they are not even malevolent in the traditional sense. They are, instead, survivors of a time when Earth was not yet Earth as we know it. Their story, as told through murals discovered in the ruins, is both wondrous and terrifying. It is the history of our planet, rewritten through a cosmic lens.

Lovecraft's imagination was scientific in its scope. He posits not just one alien race, but an evolutionary timeline spanning eons, complete with rebellion, decay, and forgotten epochs. The Shoggoths—shapeless, protean masses bred to serve the Elder Things—eventually become uncontrollable, rising up against their creators and foreshadowing a recurring theme in Lovecraft's work: the inevitable collapse of even the most advanced civilizations. What happened to the Elder Things could happen to us, and in fact, may already be happening.

The Shoggoths themselves represent perhaps the most primal horror in the story. Their origin as artificial slaves that gained sentience and rebelled is Lovecraft's dark spin on the Frankenstein myth. These creatures are not only horrifying because of their appearance or strength, but because they are a living metaphor for knowledge turned against its source. Their wordless mimicry of their creators' language—"Tekeli-li! Tekeli-li!"—is one of the most chilling moments in the novella. It is not just a cry; it is an echo of lost mastery, of language repeated without meaning, of civilization reduced to reflex.

Lovecraft's descriptions of the ruined city, carved into impossible angles and dimensions, are some of the most evocative in all of horror literature. He uses negative space, geometry, and scale to evoke unease. The city is too large, too ancient, too alien to be fully comprehended. It is not built for human bodies or minds. The explorers move through it like insects crawling through the bones of a god. And in doing so, they uncover truths about life, history, and the nature of the universe that leave them spiritually shattered.

At its core, At the Mountains of Madness is a story about human vulnerability—not to violence, but to knowledge. It asks what happens when we succeed in our pursuit of truth, when we finally lift the veil and see what lies beyond. Lovecraft's answer is clear: madness. Not because the truth is malicious, but because it is too vast. The universe is not waiting for us. It does not care. And that indifference is the true horror.

The Legacy of Madness: Modern Relevance and Literary Significance

At the Mountains of Madness is perhaps Lovecraft's most cinematic story, despite the fact that it has never been properly adapted to the screen. Its scale, its structure, and its combination of horror and science fiction have influenced generations of filmmakers, authors, and game designers. From John Carpenter's The Thing to Ridley Scott's Prometheus, echoes of Lovecraft's Antarctic horrors reverberate throughout modern pop culture.

And yet, despite its scope, the story remains deeply personal. It is the narrative of one man trying—and failing—to warn a world that does not wish to listen.

The novella is also Lovecraft's most fully realized example of "non-Euclidean horror"—a term often used to describe his portrayal of physical and metaphysical spaces that defy human logic. This is not mere fantasy. It is rooted in the philosophical movements of Lovecraft's time, particularly the rise of non-Euclidean geometry and quantum mechanics. Lovecraft, though not a scientist, understood the cultural implications of these fields. They suggested that the universe was not fixed or simple, but complex, fluid, and ultimately unknowable. His fiction became the artistic embodiment of these ideas.

This modern translation seeks to preserve the awe and terror of Lovecraft's original while making his dense and archaic prose more accessible to contemporary readers. Lovecraft's style, though elegant and evocative, often employs convoluted syntax, excessive adjectives, and archaic vocabulary.

These features, while atmospheric, can distance readers from the emotional immediacy of the story. In this edition, the language has been carefully modernized for clarity and flow, without compromising the tone, content, or structure. The goal is to allow today's reader to immerse fully in the narrative—to feel its creeping dread, its revelations, and its final, shattering truths.

Reading At the Mountains of Madness today is more than reading a horror story—it is an intellectual challenge, a philosophical confrontation, and a reflection on the dangers of human arrogance. It forces us to consider whether we are prepared for what lies beneath the surface of things—whether scientific discovery, technological advancement, or even personal ambition might lead us not to glory, but to horror. Lovecraft's Antarctic city is not just a ruin. It is a mirror, showing us what we might become if we forget our limits.

In a time when humanity is once again pushing into the unknown—into space, into the genome, into artificial intelligence—Lovecraft's warning remains timely. We may find wonders. We may find truths. But we may also awaken ancient fears, buried not in the ice, but in the very structure of reality.

This edition invites you to walk alongside Dr. Dyer, into the coldest place on Earth and into the most fragile corners of the human mind. What you find there may shake you. But once you've seen it, you cannot look away. The mountains are not merely mountains. The madness is not merely metaphor. And some doors, once opened, can never be closed.

Chapter I

I am speaking out because scientists have ignored my warnings, refusing to listen without knowing the reasons behind them. I do not want to share this information, but I feel I have no choice. I strongly oppose this planned expedition to Antarctica, with its large-scale drilling and melting of the ancient ice caps, yet I fear my warning will be ignored.

I know many will doubt what I say. My story will seem unbelievable, but if I leave out the strangest parts, there would be nothing left to tell. I do have proof—photographs taken from the ground and the air—though even these might be dismissed as fakes. The drawings we made will likely be ridiculed, even though their details should puzzle any expert who looks at them.

In the end, I must rely on a few open-minded scientists—those willing to judge my evidence on its own shocking merits or compare it with ancient myths that may hold deeper truths. If these experts have enough influence, perhaps they can convince others not to make reckless choices in that terrible land—the place I now call the Mountains of Madness.

Unfortunately, my colleagues and I are not well-known figures in the scientific community. We are from a small university, and people rarely take unknown researchers seriously, especially when they bring forward something strange and controversial. It also works against us that we are not specialists in the areas that became most important during our journey. As a geologist, my only goal in leading the Miskatonic University Expedition was to collect deep rock and soil samples from Antarctica, using a powerful new drill created by Professor Frank H. Pabodie from our engineering department.

I never intended to explore beyond my own field, but I hoped this new drilling machine would allow us to reach materials that had never been uncovered before. The drill, as the public already knows from our reports, was a groundbreaking invention. It was lightweight, easy to transport, and could drill through different layers of rock and soil faster than older methods. It combined the technology of an Artesian well drill with a circular rock drill, allowing us to dig deep with minimal equipment.

The setup included a steel drill head, jointed rods, a gasoline-powered motor, a collapsible wooden frame, dynamite for breaking tough rock, and special tools for removing debris. All of this fit onto three dog sleds, made possible by Pabodie's clever use of an aluminum alloy to reduce weight.

We also had four large Dornier airplanes, specially designed to handle the extreme altitudes of the Antarctic plateau. Pabodie had added fuel-warming systems and quick-starting devices to make sure they worked in the freezing temperatures. These planes allowed us to travel quickly between our base near the ice barrier and deeper inland locations. Once we reached new sites, our sled dogs would take over to transport supplies.

Our plan was to explore as much of Antarctica as possible in a single season—longer if necessary. We focused mainly on the mountain ranges and plateaus south of the Ross Sea, areas previously studied to different extents by famous explorers like Shackleton, Amundsen, Scott, and Byrd. By frequently relocating our camps using airplanes, we hoped to collect an extraordinary number of samples, especially from the ancient rock layers that held the oldest geological secrets.

We also wanted to gather a wide range of fossils from higher rock layers. Scientists already know that Antarctica was once much warmer, even tropical, and full of plant and animal life. Today, only a few forms of life remain, such as lichens, sea creatures, spiders, and penguins along the northern coast. Our goal was to expand this knowledge with more details and clearer evidence.

Whenever we found fossils in our drill samples, we planned to blast open the ground to extract larger, well-preserved specimens. Our drill depths would vary depending on the land conditions, but we would only dig in exposed areas—usually slopes and ridges—since the lower regions were buried under one to two miles of solid ice.

We couldn't afford to waste our drilling on thick glaciers. However, Pabodie had developed a method to melt ice using copper electrodes powered by a gasoline-driven generator. We tested this technique on a small scale during our trip, but we did not have the resources to use it fully.

Now, another expedition—the Starkweather-Moore team—plans to go back and follow this melting technique, ignoring the warnings I have given since returning from Antarctica.

***

The public kept up with the Miskatonic Expedition through our radio updates to the Arkham Advertiser and the Associated Press, along with later articles written by Pabodie and me. Our team was made up of four professors from the university—Pabodie, Lake from the biology department, Atwood from the physics department (who also specialized in meteorology), and me as the geology expert and leader of the expedition. In addition, we had sixteen assistants, including seven graduate students from Miskatonic and nine skilled mechanics.

Out of these sixteen assistants, twelve were trained pilots, and ten were skilled in using radio equipment. Eight knew how to navigate using a compass and sextant, as did Pabodie, Atwood, and I. Additionally, our two ships—both former whaling vessels reinforced for ice conditions and powered by auxiliary steam—were fully staffed with experienced crews.

The expedition was funded mainly by the Nathaniel Derby Pickman Foundation, with some extra contributions. Thanks to this financial support, we were able to prepare thoroughly, even though our mission didn't receive much public attention.

All of our supplies—including dogs, sleds, machinery, camp materials, and the unassembled parts of five airplanes—were shipped to Boston, where our ships were loaded. We were well-prepared for our mission, following the example of many skilled explorers before us. In fact, so many famous expeditions had gone before us that our own, despite its size and ambition, didn't attract much notice from the world.

As reported in the newspapers, we set sail from Boston Harbor on September 2, 1930. We took our time, sailing down the coast, passing through the Panama Canal, and stopping at Samoa and Hobart, Tasmania, where we picked up our final supplies.

None of us had ever been to the polar regions before, so we relied heavily on our ship captains—J. B. Douglas, who commanded the Arkham and led the sea voyage, and Georg Thorfinnssen, captain of the Miskatonic. Both were experienced whalers who had spent years in Antarctic waters.

As we left the civilized world behind, the sun sank lower in the northern sky each day, staying above the horizon for longer periods. Around 62° South Latitude, we spotted our first icebergs—huge, flat-topped structures with steep, vertical sides. Just before crossing the Antarctic Circle on October 20, we ran into thick field ice, which slowed us down.

After traveling through the tropics, the drop in temperature was difficult for me, but I prepared myself for the even harsher cold ahead. The strange atmospheric effects fascinated me, especially a vivid mirage—the first I had ever seen—which made distant icebergs look like towering castles from another world.

Fortunately, the ice was not too thick or tightly packed, and we were able to push through to open water at 67° South Latitude, 175° East Longitude. On the morning of October 26, we saw a bright glow in the sky, a "land blink," which meant that ice-covered land was nearby. By noon, we felt a wave of excitement as we spotted a vast, snow-covered mountain range stretching across the horizon. At last, we had reached the edge of the unknown continent, a frozen and mysterious world.

The towering peaks in front of us were clearly part of the Admiralty Range, first discovered by the explorer James Clark Ross. Our next goal was to round Cape Adare and follow the east coast of Victoria Land until we reached our planned base at McMurdo Sound, near the base of the volcano Mount Erebus at 77° 9′ South Latitude.

***

The final stretch of our journey was unforgettable, filling our minds with wonder. Tall, empty mountains rose constantly in the west, their peaks mysterious and untouched. The low northern sun at noon and the even lower southern sun at midnight cast a hazy, reddish glow over the white snow, blue ice, and dark patches of exposed rock.

Strong, unpredictable winds howled through the icy peaks, sometimes sounding like eerie music carried on the air. The strange tones made me uneasy, as if they triggered some forgotten memory. Something about the scene reminded me of the haunting Asian paintings by Nicholas Roerich, and even more disturbingly, of the eerie descriptions of the forbidden Plateau of Leng found in the dreadful Necronomicon. I later regretted ever reading that book in the university library.

On November 7th, we briefly lost sight of the western mountain range as we passed Franklin Island. The next day, we spotted the volcanic peaks of Mount Erebus and Mount Terror on Ross Island, with the long stretch of the Parry Mountains in the distance. To the east, the massive ice barrier appeared—an immense, solid wall of ice rising 200 feet high, like the towering cliffs of Quebec. This marked the furthest point we could sail south.

That afternoon, we entered McMurdo Sound and took shelter from the winds in the shadow of Mount Erebus. The active volcano stood at 12,700 feet, its rugged slopes covered in black volcanic rock. It reminded me of a Japanese painting of Mount Fuji. Beyond it, the ghostly white peak of Mount Terror loomed, standing at 10,900 feet, now long extinct. Smoke puffed from Erebus at times, and Danforth, one of our brightest graduate assistants, pointed out what looked like lava on the snowy slopes. He noted that this volcano, discovered in 1840, had likely inspired Edgar Allan Poe when he wrote:

"—the lava that flows without rest,
Its burning streams pouring down Yaanek,
In the farthest, coldest lands—

Groaning as it rolls down Mount Yaanek,
In the frozen reaches of the polar world."

Danforth was well-read and often talked about Poe, which caught my interest since Poe's only full-length novel, The Narrative of Arthur Gordon Pym, also took place in Antarctica.

On the barren shore and along the towering ice barrier behind it, flocks of strange-looking penguins squawked and flapped their wings, while seals swam in the water or lounged on drifting ice.

Using small boats, we struggled to land on Ross Island shortly after midnight on November 9th. We secured thick cables from the ships to the shore and prepared to unload our supplies using a pulley system.

Setting foot on Antarctic land for the first time was an overwhelming experience, stirring deep and complicated emotions, even though earlier expeditions by Scott and Shackleton had already explored this place.

Our first camp on the frozen coast, at the base of the volcano, was temporary. The Arkham remained our main base. We unloaded all of our essential equipment, including drilling gear, sled dogs, tents, food, gasoline, a special device for melting ice, cameras for both standard and aerial photography, airplane parts, and other important supplies. We also brought three small portable radios—on top of the ones in the planes—so we could communicate with the Arkham from anywhere we traveled across the Antarctic continent.

The ship's larger radio system allowed us to send updates to the Arkham Advertiser's powerful station in Kingsport Head, Massachusetts. Our plan was to finish our research in a single Antarctic summer, but if necessary, we were prepared to stay through the winter.

In that case, the Miskatonic would sail north before the ice froze over to bring back supplies for another season of exploration.

***

I don't need to repeat what the newspapers have already reported about our early work—our climb up Mt. Erebus, the successful drilling for minerals at multiple sites on Ross Island, and how quickly Pabodie's machine worked, even through solid rock. They also covered our first test of the small ice-melting device, our difficult climb up the massive ice barrier with sleds and supplies, and the final assembly of our five large airplanes at the camp on top of the barrier.

Our team of twenty men and fifty-five Alaskan sled dogs stayed in excellent health. So far, we had not faced extreme cold or dangerous storms. The temperature usually stayed between zero and 25 degrees Fahrenheit, which wasn't much different from New England winters we had experienced before. Our camp at the ice barrier was set up to store gasoline, food, explosives, and other supplies.

We only needed four planes to carry our exploration gear. The fifth plane was left behind with a pilot and two crew members from the ships. This way, if something happened to our planes, they could still reach us from the Arkham. Later, when we weren't using all four planes for transportation, we planned to fly one or two back and forth between this supply base and another camp about 600 to 700 miles farther south, beyond Beardmore Glacier.

Even though explorers before us had warned of terrifying winds that rushed down from the plateau, we decided not to set up smaller supply bases along the way. We wanted to save time and resources, even if it meant taking a risk.

Our wireless reports spoke of the breathtaking four-hour, nonstop flight we made on November 21st. We soared over towering ice shelves, with massive peaks rising in the west and the endless silence of Antarctica broken only by the sound of our engines. Strong winds gave us only minor trouble, and when we hit thick fog, our radio compasses guided us safely. As we approached a huge rise in the land between latitudes 83° and 84°, we knew we had reached Beardmore Glacier—the world's largest valley glacier. The frozen sea now gave way to a dark, mountainous coastline.

At last, we had entered the untouched, lifeless world of the far south. As we realized this, we saw Mt. Nansen rising in the distance to the east, nearly 15,000 feet tall.

The successful setup of our southern base above the glacier, at latitude 86° 7' and longitude 174° 23', became part of history. So did our fast and effective drilling and blasting at various locations, which we reached by sled or short flights. Another major achievement was Pabodie's team, which included graduate students Gedney and Carroll, climbing Mt. Nansen between December 13th and 15th.

We were about 8,500 feet above sea level. Our test drillings showed that in some spots, solid ground was only 12 feet beneath the ice. We used the ice-melting device frequently, drilling deep into the ground and setting off explosives to collect rock samples from places no explorer had ever studied before.

The ancient granites and sandstone we found confirmed our belief that this plateau was connected to most of the continent west of us. However, it seemed different from the land east of South America. At the time, we thought that area might be a separate, smaller continent, joined to the larger one by frozen waters between the Ross and Weddell Seas. Later, Byrd's research proved that idea wrong.

In some of the sandstone we blasted open, we found fascinating fossil markings and fragments. These included ferns, seaweed, trilobites, crinoids, and mollusks like linguellae and gastropods. These fossils were important because they helped reveal the ancient history of the region.

There was also one unusual find—a strange, triangular marking with ridges, about a foot across. Lake put it together from three broken pieces of slate found west near the Queen Alexandra Range. As a biologist, he found the markings incredibly mysterious and intriguing. However, to me as a geologist, it looked like a natural ripple effect often seen in sedimentary rocks.

Since slate forms when layers of sedimentary rock are pressed together over time, any patterns in the original rock can get distorted under pressure. Because of this, I didn't think the striations were anything too surprising.

***

On January 6, 1931, Lake, Pabodie, Daniels, six students, four mechanics, and I flew over the South Pole in two large planes. At one point, a powerful wind forced us to land, but thankfully, it didn't develop into a full storm. As the newspapers mentioned, this was just one of several flights we took to explore areas that other expeditions had not yet reached.

At first, our flights were disappointing because we didn't find many new geographical features. However, we did witness incredible mirages, similar to the ones we had seen on our sea voyage. Distant mountains appeared to float in the air like magical cities, and at times, the entire frozen landscape seemed to transform into a golden, silver, and red dreamland under the glow of the low midnight sun.

Flying on cloudy days was much more challenging. The snow-covered ground and the overcast sky often blended together into a strange, glowing whiteness, making it hard to tell where the horizon was.

Eventually, we decided to move forward with our original plan: flying 500 miles east with all four planes to set up a new sub-base. We believed this area was part of a smaller, separate continent, though we later realized we were wrong. Collecting geological samples from this region would be useful for comparing them with what we had already found.

So far, we had stayed in excellent health. Drinking lime juice helped prevent scurvy, and since temperatures mostly stayed above zero, we didn't always need to wear our heaviest furs. It was now midsummer in Antarctica, and if we worked quickly, we hoped to finish by March and avoid having to stay through the long, harsh winter.

Several violent windstorms had hit us from the west, but thanks to Atwood's skill in building simple airplane shelters and windbreaks from heavy snow blocks, we avoided any serious damage. He also reinforced our main camp buildings with packed snow, making them sturdier. Everything had gone surprisingly well, almost too well.

The outside world was aware of our plans, including Lake's unexpected decision to explore westward—or more precisely, northwest—before we moved to our new base. For some reason, he was deeply fixated on the strange, ridged triangular marking in the slate we had found earlier. He studied it obsessively, interpreting it in ways that went against normal scientific understanding. His curiosity drove him to insist on drilling and blasting in the rock formations to the west, where the fragments had originally come from.

Lake became convinced that the marking was made by a large, unknown creature that didn't fit into any known classification. He believed it was highly evolved, even though the rock it was found in was unimaginably old. The age of the rock, possibly from the Cambrian or even pre-Cambrian period, suggested that no complex life forms should have existed at that time—only simple single-celled organisms or, at most, trilobites. If Lake was right, this fossil was between 500 million and a billion years old.

Chapter II

I could tell that the public was fascinated by our radio updates about Lake's journey northwest into unexplored regions, though we didn't mention his ambitious hopes of changing everything we knew about biology and geology.

From January 11th to 18th, Lake, Pabodie, and five others went on a sledding and drilling trip. They lost two dogs when crossing a large pressure ridge in the ice, but they brought back more samples of ancient slate rock. Even I was intrigued by the large number of fossil-like markings in this incredibly old layer of rock. However, these fossils appeared to be from very simple life forms, and while it was unusual for any fossils to exist in such ancient rock, I still didn't understand why Lake was so determined to change our schedule. His plan would require all four planes, many of our men, and almost all of our equipment.

In the end, I didn't refuse his request, though I chose not to go with them despite Lake asking for my geological expertise. While they were away, I stayed at the base with Pabodie and five others to finalize plans for our move eastward. One of the planes had started transporting extra gasoline from McMurdo Sound for the next phase of our work, but that could be put on hold. I kept one sled and nine dogs with me, since in a place as empty and lifeless as this, it was dangerous to be stranded without transportation.

Lake's group sent regular reports from their planes' shortwave radios, which we picked up at our base and relayed to the Arkham at McMurdo Sound. From there, the messages were sent out to the world.

They left on January 22nd at 4 a.m., and two hours later, we received the first radio message. Lake reported that they were landing and preparing to drill a test hole about 300 miles away. Six hours later, he sent another, much more excited message. His team had dug and blasted a shallow pit, uncovering slate fragments with markings similar to the ones that had puzzled him before.

Three hours after that, he sent another update, saying they were continuing their flight despite strong winds. When I sent a message warning him about the risk, he simply replied that his latest discoveries were worth any danger.

I could tell he was too excited to listen to reason, and there was nothing I could do to stop him. Still, the thought of him flying further into that endless, storm-filled, and mysterious white landscape—one that stretched 1,500 miles to the barely known coast of Queen Mary and Knox Lands—was deeply unsettling.

***

About an hour and a half later, we received another message from Lake's plane. This time, he sounded even more excited, and for a moment, I wished I had gone with them.

"10:05 p.m. Still flying. After the snowstorm, we've spotted a mountain range ahead—higher than anything we've ever seen before. Might be as tall as the Himalayas when factoring in the height of the plateau. Estimated position: Latitude 76° 15', Longitude 113° 10' E. The range stretches as far as we can see in both directions. We think we see two smoking peaks. All the mountaintops are black and bare of snow. Strong winds from the peaks are making flying difficult."

Pabodie, the men, and I were glued to the radio, barely breathing as we listened. The thought of a massive, unknown mountain range

700 miles away filled us with excitement. Even if we weren't there ourselves, our expedition had discovered something incredible.

Thirty minutes later, Lake called again:

"Moulton's plane was forced to land on the plateau near the foothills. No one is hurt, and we might be able to fix it. For now, we're moving the necessary equipment to the other three planes so we can return or continue as needed. We won't need to fly any more large planes for now. These mountains are beyond anything we ever imagined. I'm taking Carroll's plane up for scouting with all unnecessary weight removed.

"You can't imagine what we're seeing. Some peaks must be over 35,000 feet high—higher than Everest. Atwood is going to measure the height while Carroll and I fly up. I might have been wrong about the smoking cones. The rock layers look like they've been stacked in layers, possibly pre-Cambrian slate mixed with other materials. The mountain ridges are strange—some peaks have sections that look like giant cubes stacked together. The whole landscape is glowing in the red-gold light of the low sun. It looks like something out of a dream—like a gateway to an unknown world. I wish you were here to see it."

Even though it was technically time to sleep, none of us even considered going to bed. I imagined it was the same at McMurdo Sound, where the Arkham and the supply camp were also receiving these messages. Captain Douglas radioed his congratulations on the discovery, and Sherman, the radio operator at the cache, added his excitement. We were all a little worried about the damaged plane, but we hoped it could be repaired.

Then, at 11 p.m., another message came in:

"Carroll and I are flying over the tallest foothills. We can't try the highest peaks in this weather, but we will later. Climbing is extremely difficult at this altitude, but it's worth it. The range is solid rock, so we can't see what's beyond it. The main peaks are taller than the Himalayas, and they look bizarre. The rock seems to be mostly pre-Cambrian slate, but many layers have been pushed up over time. There are no signs of volcanic activity. The range stretches farther than we can see, and above 21,000 feet, the slopes are completely clear of snow.

"There are strange shapes on the mountainsides—huge square blocks with vertical walls. In some areas, they form rectangular walls, like ancient castles in old Asian paintings. From a distance, they are incredible. When we flew closer, Carroll thought they were made up of smaller pieces, but it might just be weathering. Most of the edges are crumbling and worn down, as if they've been exposed to the elements for millions of years.

"The upper parts seem to be made of a different type of rock, lighter than anything we've seen on the lower slopes. It's probably crystalline in origin. We saw a lot of cave openings, some perfectly square or semicircular. You need to come check this out. I think I saw a flat structure on top of one peak. Right now, we're at 21,500 feet, and the tallest peaks are probably between 30,000 and 35,000 feet high. It's bitterly cold, and the wind is howling through the valleys and caves, making eerie whistling sounds. But so far, flying conditions are okay."

For the next thirty minutes, Lake kept sending updates, describing the mountains and saying he planned to climb some of the peaks on foot. I radioed back, telling him I would join him as soon as he could send a plane for me. Pabodie and I started figuring out how to move enough gasoline to support this unexpected part of the expedition.

Lake's drilling and flights would need a lot of fuel, so we had to prioritize getting supplies to his new base at the foot of the mountains.

I contacted Captain Douglas, asking him to get as much fuel and supplies from the ships as possible and bring them up the ice barrier using the last dog team. We needed to establish a direct route between McMurdo Sound and Lake's location.

Later, Lake called again to say he had decided to keep the camp where Moulton's plane had landed, since repairs were already underway. The ice sheet there was thin, and patches of dark ground were visible. He planned to drill and blast in that area before starting any climbing trips or sledge journeys.

He ended the message by describing how overwhelming the landscape felt. He spoke about the towering, silent peaks rising like a giant wall against the sky, making him feel as if he were standing at the edge of the world.

Atwood's measurements showed that the five tallest peaks ranged between 30,000 and 34,000 feet high.

The harsh, windswept landscape unsettled Lake, as it suggested that the area was sometimes hit by incredibly strong storms—far worse than anything we had experienced so far. His camp was just over five miles from where the steep foothills began to rise.

I could sense a hint of unease in his messages, sent across the vast, icy distance of 700 miles. He urged us to move quickly and finish exploring this strange new area as soon as possible. After working nonstop at an incredible pace all day, he was finally going to rest.

It was a strange feeling—standing in the shadow of towering, silent peaks that rose like a massive wall stretching up to the edge of the sky.

***

That morning, I had a three-way radio conversation with Lake and Captain Douglas, who were at their separate bases. We decided that one of Lake's planes would come to my base to pick up Pabodie, the five men with us, and as much fuel as it could carry. The rest of the fuel supply, depending on whether we went east, could be figured out later. For now, Lake had enough to keep his camp running and continue drilling.

At some point, we would need to resupply our old base in the south, but if we canceled the trip east, we wouldn't need it again until the next summer. In the meantime, Lake planned to send a plane to find a direct route between his new mountain camp and McMurdo Sound.

Pabodie and I got ready to shut down our base, whether for a short break or permanently. If we had to stay in Antarctica through the winter, we would probably fly straight from Lake's camp to the Arkham without coming back here. Some of our tents had already been reinforced with blocks of packed snow, so we decided to finish the job and turn the camp into a more permanent shelter. Since we had plenty of extra tents, Lake had enough for his team even after we arrived. I sent a message confirming that Pabodie and I would be ready to head northwest after another full day of work and a night's rest.

However, after 4 p.m., we became distracted from our tasks because Lake started sending frantic and excited messages. His day had not started well—an aerial survey of the nearby exposed rock revealed that the ancient rock layers he had been searching for were completely missing. These were the layers that made up the massive peaks towering in the distance, but none of them were visible near his camp.

Most of the rocks in the area appeared to be from much younger geological periods, mostly Jurassic and Comanchean sandstone, along with some Permian and Triassic schist. Occasionally, they spotted glossy black outcroppings that looked like hard, slate-like coal.

This discovery frustrated Lake since his entire plan depended on finding rock samples that were over 500 million years old. He realized that to reach the ancient slate where he had discovered the strange markings, he would have to take a long sledge journey from the foothills to the steep slopes of the towering mountains.

Despite this setback, Lake still planned to carry out some drilling in the area as part of the expedition's overall research. He set up the drill and assigned five men to operate it, while the rest of the team worked on setting up camp and repairing the damaged airplane.

They chose a section of sandstone about a quarter of a mile from camp as their first drilling site, since it was the softest exposed rock in the area. The drill worked smoothly, making progress without needing much extra blasting.

Then, about three hours later, after they set off the first powerful explosion, the drill crew suddenly began shouting. Young Gedney, who was acting as the foreman, ran back to camp with shocking news.

***

They had discovered a cave. While drilling, they first hit sandstone, but soon reached a layer of Comanchean limestone filled with tiny fossils of ancient sea creatures like corals, shellfish, and spiny echinoderms. Some signs of fossilized fish bones, likely from sharks and other prehistoric species, were also found. This was already an exciting discovery, as it was the first evidence of vertebrate fossils the expedition had uncovered. But then, something even more surprising happened—the drill suddenly broke through into empty space.

A powerful blast revealed the underground secret. Now, through a jagged hole about five feet wide and three feet thick, the team could see into a shallow limestone cavern. This underground space had been hollowed out by water more than fifty million years ago when the world was much warmer and covered in tropical forests.

The cave wasn't very deep, only about seven or eight feet, but it stretched out in all directions. A faint movement of air suggested that it was part of a much larger underground system. The ceiling and floor were lined with massive stalactites and stalagmites, with some joining together to form stone columns.

But the most astonishing discovery was the huge amount of shells and bones filling parts of the cave. It seemed that ancient rivers had washed remains from prehistoric jungles and forests into this underground space, leaving behind fossils from many different time periods. The collection of creatures found there was more than any paleontologist could study in a lifetime. There were fossils of mollusks, crustaceans, fish, amphibians, reptiles, birds, and early mammals—some familiar and some completely unknown.

It was no surprise that Gedney ran back to the camp shouting, or that everyone else dropped what they were doing and rushed through the freezing cold to see this incredible discovery. The towering drilling rig now stood as a gateway to the hidden past of the Earth.

Once Lake had taken a closer look, he quickly wrote a note and sent young Moulton back to camp to send a radio message. This was how I first learned about the discovery. His message described early shells, bones from ancient armored fish, pieces of giant marine reptiles like mosasaurs, dinosaur bones, pterodactyl teeth and wing fragments, fossils of early birds, and even skeletons of primitive mammals such as early horses, ancient rhino-like creatures, and other prehistoric species.

There were no fossils of more recent animals like mastodons, elephants, camels, deer, or cattle. Because of this, Lake concluded that the last creatures in this cave had lived during the Oligocene period, and that the cavern had been sealed off from the surface for at least thirty million years.

But the most puzzling thing was how many very old fossils were mixed in with the younger ones. The limestone layer itself clearly belonged to the Comanchean period, proven by embedded fossils that matched that age. However, the loose fossils inside the cave included some that should have come from much older periods—hundreds of millions of years earlier—including early fish, mollusks, and corals from the Silurian and Ordovician ages.

The only explanation was that this part of the world had somehow kept ancient life forms alive for much longer than expected. Normally, species disappear over time, replaced by newer ones, but here, it seemed that animals from over 300 million years ago had survived alongside creatures from just 30 million years ago. How long this pattern continued before the cave was sealed was impossible to guess.

Eventually, though, the arrival of the great ice sheets during the Pleistocene—only about 500,000 years ago, a blink of an eye compared to the cave's age—must have wiped out whatever ancient creatures had managed to survive until then.

***

Lake wasn't satisfied with just one message. Before Moulton even returned to camp, he sent another report, which was quickly delivered across the snow. After that, Moulton remained at the wireless station in one of the planes, continuously transmitting updates from Lake to me and the Arkham, which then relayed them to the outside world.

Anyone who followed the newspapers at the time would remember how much excitement these reports caused among scientists. In fact, they eventually led to the Starkweather-Moore Expedition—the very one I am now desperately trying to stop.

It's best if I repeat Lake's messages exactly as they were sent and translated by our radio operator, McTighe, who wrote them down in shorthand:

Fowler has made a major discovery in the sandstone and limestone fragments from our blasting. He found several clear triangular markings just like the ones we saw in the ancient slate. This proves that the same life form existed from more than 600 million years ago all the way to the Comanchean period, with only minor changes in shape and a slight reduction in size. In fact, the Comanchean markings seem even more primitive or worn down than the older ones.

This discovery is incredibly important. It could change biology as much as Einstein changed math and physics. It builds on my previous research and supports my earlier conclusions.

It seems to confirm what I suspected—that Earth went through at least one entire cycle of life before the one we already know, which began with ancient single-celled organisms. These life forms must have evolved and developed at least a billion years ago, when the planet was still young and too harsh for any normal living things.

Now the big question is: when, where, and how did this unknown stage of life take place?

***

Later, while studying some skeletal fragments from large land and sea reptiles, as well as early mammals, we found strange injuries on the bones. These wounds didn't match the bite marks or damage caused by any known predator from any time period.

There were two types of injuries—some were deep, straight holes, while others looked like rough cuts or slashes. In one or two cases, bones had been completely and cleanly severed. However, only a few of the specimens showed these marks.

I've sent a request to the camp for electric torches so we can continue our search deeper underground. We plan to break away some of the stalactites to explore further.

***

Later on, we discovered a strange piece of soapstone about six inches wide and an inch and a half thick. It looked completely different from any of the local rock formations. The stone had a greenish color, but there was no clear way to determine how old it was.

Its surface was unusually smooth and well-shaped, resembling a five-pointed star with its tips broken off. There were also signs that it had been split or chipped at the inner angles and the center of its surface. In the middle of the unbroken side, we noticed a small, smooth dent.

The stone sparked a lot of curiosity about where it came from and how it had been shaped over time. It might have been worn down by water, though we weren't sure. Carroll, using a magnifying glass, thought he could see tiny markings in a pattern, possibly important for studying the geology of the area.

Strangely, the dogs became restless as we examined the stone, almost as if they could sense something unsettling about it. They clearly disliked it. We decided to check if it had any kind of scent that might explain their reaction.

I'll send another report once Mills returns with a light and we begin exploring the underground section.

***

10:15 p.m. Major discovery. Orrendorf and Watkins, while working underground with lights at 9:45, found a massive, barrel-shaped fossil of a completely unknown type. It is likely some kind of plant unless it's an overgrown version of an unfamiliar sea creature. The tissue seems to have been preserved by mineral salts. It is tough like leather but still surprisingly flexible in some spots.

There are clear signs that parts of it broke off at both ends and along the sides. The fossil is six feet long, with a central width of about three and a half feet, tapering down to just one foot at each end. It looks like a barrel, but instead of wooden slats, it has five thick, bulging ridges running along its length.

At the middle of these ridges, there are breaks where thinner stalk-like structures seem to have snapped off. Between the ridges, strange comb-like or wing-like structures are folded up, though they can also spread out like fans. Most of these are badly damaged, but one is almost fully intact, showing a wingspan of nearly seven feet. The way these parts are arranged is oddly similar to creatures described in ancient myths, especially the so-called "Elder Things" mentioned in the Necronomicon.

The wings appear to be made of a thin membrane stretched over a framework of tube-like structures, possibly glands. Tiny holes can be seen at the tips of these tubes. The ends of the body are shriveled, making it impossible to tell what might have been broken off there. We will dissect it when we return to camp to determine whether it was a plant or an animal. Many of its features look extremely primitive, almost unbelievably ancient.

Everyone is now cutting away stalactites and searching for more specimens. We've also found more bones with unusual markings, but those will have to wait. The dogs are reacting badly to the discovery.

They seem terrified of the fossil and would probably destroy it if we didn't keep it away from them.

***

11:30 p.m. Urgent message. Dyer, Pabodie, Douglas—this is of the highest importance. Arkham must send this to Kingsport Head Station immediately. The strange barrel-shaped fossil is the ancient creature that left those prints in the rock. Mills, Boudreau, and Fowler found thirteen more of them underground, about forty feet from the opening. They were mixed with small, smooth soapstone fragments, shaped like stars, though these show no breaks except at some points.

Out of the organic specimens, eight seem to be in perfect condition, with all their parts intact. We've brought them to the surface, keeping the dogs far away—they can't stand being near these things. Listen carefully and confirm the details so that the newspapers get everything right.

These creatures are eight feet long. Their barrel-like bodies are six feet long and have five ridges along the sides. The widest part is three and a half feet across, tapering down to a foot at both ends. The skin is dark gray, flexible, and extremely tough. They have seven-foot-long, membranous wings of the same dark gray color, folded into the furrows between the ridges. The wing structure seems to be tubular or glandular, with small openings at the tips, and the edges of the wings have a serrated shape.

Around the middle of the body, at the top of each of the five ridges, are five sets of light-gray, flexible arms or tentacles. These were found folded tightly against the body, but they can stretch out over three feet long. They resemble the arms of a primitive sea lily. Each main arm is three inches thick at the base, then splits into five smaller branches after six inches. Each of those branches divides again after eight inches into five small, tapering tendrils, making a total of twenty-five tentacles per arm.

At the top of the body is a short, rounded neck that is a lighter shade of gray and appears to have gill-like features. It connects to a five-pointed, star-shaped head covered in tiny, wiry bristles of different shimmering colors. The head is thick and puffy, about two feet from point to point, with five short, flexible yellowish tubes sticking out from each point. In the center of the head is a slit, likely used for breathing. At the end of each tube is a round expansion where a yellow membrane can be pulled back, revealing a glassy, red-irised eye.

There are also five slightly longer reddish tubes at the inner angles of the star-shaped head. These end in sac-like swellings that, when pressed, open into bell-shaped mouths lined with sharp, white tooth-like structures. All of these tubes, bristles, and head points were folded tightly down against the body when found. Despite their leathery toughness, they are surprisingly flexible.

At the bottom of the body, there is a similar star-shaped structure. A bulbous, light-gray section—like a neck but without gill-like features—connects to a greenish five-pointed shape.

The lower part of the body has strong, four-foot-long muscular arms that taper from seven inches wide at the base to about two and a half inches at the tip. At the end of each arm is a greenish, triangular, paddle-like fin with five veins, measuring eight inches long and six inches wide. These are likely the structures that made the ancient footprints found in rock layers dating from a billion to sixty million years ago.

There are also two-foot-long reddish tubes sticking out from the inner angles of the lower star-shaped section. These tubes taper from three inches wide at the base to one inch at the tip, with small openings at the ends. Every part of the creature is both incredibly tough and highly flexible. The four-foot-long arms with the paddles seem built for movement, possibly in water or on land. When touched, they seem to suggest powerful muscles.

We still can't say for sure whether these things are plants or animals, but right now, it seems more likely they're animals. They may be a highly evolved type of ancient sea creature, but they still show some features of much earlier life forms. Their resemblance to echinoderms (like sea stars and sea urchins) is clear, though there are contradictions.

The wings are a mystery—if they lived in water, why would they need wings? Their symmetrical shape seems more like plants than animals, suggesting an up-and-down structure rather than the front-and-back shape typical of most creatures. The fact that they evolved so early, even before the most basic known prehistoric life, makes their origins a complete mystery.

These specimens look so much like creatures from ancient myths that it raises the question of whether they existed outside Antarctica long ago. Dyer and Pabodie have read the Necronomicon and seen Clark Ashton Smith's eerie paintings based on its descriptions, so they'll understand when I say these resemble the so-called "Elder Things" that legends claim created all life on Earth—either as a joke or by accident. Students have always assumed those stories were just imaginative takes on ancient marine creatures, but this discovery is making me reconsider. It also reminds me of the bizarre creatures mentioned in old folklore about the Cthulhu cult.

This opens up an entirely new field of study. Based on the fossils found around them, these remains probably date back to the late Cretaceous or early Eocene period. Thick stalagmites formed above them, so it took a lot of work to dig them out, but their tough structure prevented any damage. Their state of preservation is unbelievable—likely due to the limestone's chemical properties. We haven't found any more yet, but we will continue searching later. Right now, our focus is on transporting these fourteen massive specimens to the camp.

Since the dogs refuse to go near them, we'll have to move them ourselves. With nine men—leaving three behind to watch the dogs—we should be able to manage the three sleds, though the wind is bad. We also need to set up plane communication with McMurdo Sound and start transporting materials. But first, I have to dissect one of these things before we get any rest. I wish we had a real laboratory here.

Dyer should regret trying to stop my westward expedition. First, we found the tallest mountains on Earth, and now we have this. If this isn't the biggest discovery of the expedition, I don't know what is. We've just secured our place in scientific history.

Pabodie, congratulations on the drill that led us to the cave. Arkham, please confirm and repeat my description.

***

"I need to examine one of these things right away."
"First, we found the tallest mountains—now this!"

***

The excitement Pabodie and I felt after receiving this report was almost impossible to describe, and the rest of our group shared in our enthusiasm. McTighe, who had quickly translated the most important parts as they came through the radio, wrote down the full message from his shorthand notes as soon as Lake's operator finished transmitting.

Everyone understood how important this discovery was, and I immediately sent Lake my congratulations once the Arkham's operator repeated back the details, as he had requested. Sherman, stationed at the McMurdo Sound supply cache, and Captain Douglas of the Arkham followed my example. Later, as the expedition leader, I added a statement to be sent through the Arkham to the outside world.

There was no chance of sleep in the middle of such excitement, and I wanted nothing more than to get to Lake's camp as soon as possible. I was disappointed when he reported that a growing mountain storm made it too dangerous to fly right away.

However, in just an hour and a half, our excitement grew even more. Lake sent another message confirming that they had successfully moved all fourteen massive specimens to the camp. The job had been extremely difficult since the creatures were much heavier than expected, but the nine men managed to complete the task. Some of the team was now building a snow enclosure at a safe distance from the camp so the dogs could be kept there for easier feeding.

The specimens were carefully placed on the hard snow near the camp, except for one that Lake had already started to examine. However, the dissection turned out to be more difficult than he had anticipated. Despite using heat from a gasoline stove inside the newly built lab tent, the seemingly flexible outer layer of the creature remained tough and nearly impossible to cut. Lake struggled to make any cuts without causing enough damage to ruin the details he was trying to study.

Although he had seven other undamaged specimens, they were too rare to waste unless the cave contained more of them. So, he decided to work on one that was already damaged—it still had remnants of the starfish-like structures at both ends, but its main body was crushed and split open along one of its large ridges.

The results of the dissection, which he quickly sent over the radio, were shocking and confusing. The tools they had weren't sharp enough to cut the strange tissue with precision, but what little they could examine left us all stunned.

Everything we knew about biology would have to be reconsidered. This creature wasn't made of the same kind of cells that any known life-form was. There was almost no sign of fossilization, and even though it was likely around forty million years old, its internal organs were still completely intact.

Its tough, almost indestructible body seemed to be a natural part of its structure, belonging to an ancient form of evolution unlike anything we could have imagined. At first, the inside appeared dry, but as the heat from the tent caused it to thaw, a thick, dark-green liquid with a strong and unpleasant smell began to ooze from the less damaged side. It wasn't exactly blood, but it seemed to serve the same purpose.

By the time Lake reached this stage, all thirty-seven dogs had been brought to the unfinished enclosure near the camp. Even from that distance, they began barking wildly and acting restless, clearly disturbed by the sharp, spreading odor of the strange creature.

***

Instead of solving the mystery of the strange creature, the dissection only made it more confusing. The guesses about its outer body parts had been right, and based on those, it seemed clear the thing was an animal. But when Lake examined the inside, he found so many plant-like features that he was completely unsure.

The creature had a digestive system, a way to circulate fluids, and it got rid of waste through the red tubes on its starfish-shaped lower part. At first glance, it seemed to breathe oxygen rather than carbon dioxide, and there were strange signs of air-storage chambers. It even appeared to have more than one breathing system—one that used an external opening, and at least two others, possibly gills and pores.

It was obviously amphibious and seemed built to survive long periods without air, possibly in some kind of deep sleep. There were also vocal structures, but they were unlike anything known. The creature probably couldn't form words like humans, but it might have been able to make musical sounds that covered a wide range of pitches. Its muscles were surprisingly strong, almost unnaturally so.

What shocked Lake the most was its nervous system, which was incredibly advanced. While some features looked primitive and ancient, others were extremely specialized and complex. The creature had five brain lobes, showing intelligence far beyond what he expected. It also had sensory abilities unlike anything on Earth, partly linked to the wiry cilia on its head. Lake suspected it had more than the five senses humans do, meaning its behavior couldn't be compared to any known life form.

It must have been an incredibly sensitive and highly functional creature in its original world, possibly similar to ants and bees in the way it lived. It reproduced more like plants, specifically ferns, developing from spores that grew at the tips of its wings.

At this point, naming the creature felt impossible. It had some features of a starfish, but it was much more than that. It was partly plant-like but also had most of the key traits of an animal. Its body shape and other details clearly showed it had come from the ocean, yet there was no way to tell how much it had adapted over time.

The wings, despite everything, still suggested they might have been used for flying. The biggest mystery was how such a complicated creature could have evolved so early on Earth—its footprints were found in some of the oldest rocks ever known. It seemed impossible, which made Lake think of ancient myths about powerful beings from the stars that had created life on Earth, either as a joke or by mistake. He also recalled the strange folklore stories told by one of Miskatonic's English professors about creatures from beyond our world.

***

Naturally, Lake considered the idea that the ancient footprints might have come from a less-developed ancestor of the creatures they had found. But after looking at the advanced features of the older fossils, he quickly dismissed that theory. If anything, the newer specimens seemed to have declined rather than evolved into something more complex.

The paddle-like feet had shrunk, and the body structure appeared rougher and more basic. Even the nervous system and internal organs showed signs of becoming simpler over time, with many parts looking unused or leftover from something more advanced. In the end, they had more questions than answers, so Lake jokingly decided to name the creatures "The Elder Ones" after old myths.

Around 2:30 a.m., he decided to stop for the night and get some rest. He covered the dissected specimen with a tarp, stepped outside the lab tent, and looked at the other preserved specimens with new curiosity.

The constant Antarctic sun had started softening their bodies slightly, and on a few of them, the head tubes and pointed structures had begun to loosen and unfold. But since the air was still freezing, Lake wasn't worried about them decomposing too quickly. Just to be safe, he moved the untouched specimens closer together and covered them with an extra tent to block the sun. This also helped reduce their scent, which was clearly disturbing the dogs. Despite being kept far away behind growing snow walls, the animals were still uneasy and restless. More men were now working to build the walls higher to keep the dogs from getting too agitated.

Since the wind was picking up and the massive mountains looked ready to send powerful gusts their way, Lake had to weigh down the corners of the tent with heavy blocks of snow. The team had been concerned about sudden Antarctic storms before, and now they took extra precautions. Under Atwood's direction, they reinforced the tents, the new dog shelter, and the simple plane covers with snow on the side facing the mountains. These snow-built shelters had been started whenever there was extra time, but they weren't as sturdy as they needed to be. Lake finally had everyone stop what they were doing and focus on strengthening them.

By the time Lake was ready to sign off, it was past 4 a.m. He told the rest of us to get some rest, just as his team planned to do once their barriers were taller. He had a friendly chat with Pabodie over the radio, again praising the incredible drills that had helped them make their discoveries. Atwood also sent greetings and thanks.

I congratulated Lake and admitted he had been right about exploring the west. We agreed to check in by radio at 10 a.m. If the storm had died down by then, Lake would send a plane to pick up my group. Just before heading to bed, I sent one last message to the Arkham, instructing them to soften the news a bit before sharing it with the public. The full details were so shocking that people might not believe them without more proof.

Chapter III

No one got much sleep that morning. The excitement from Lake's discovery, combined with the howling wind, made it impossible to rest. The storm was already fierce where we were, but we couldn't stop thinking about how much worse it might be at Lake's camp, right beneath the towering, mysterious mountains that seemed to stir up these powerful winds.

At ten o'clock, McTighe got up and tried to reach Lake over the radio as planned, but something in the air seemed to block communication. We did manage to contact the Arkham, where Douglas told us he had also been trying to reach Lake without success. He hadn't even realized there was a storm, since McMurdo Sound was experiencing only light winds, even while it raged around us.

We spent the entire day listening and attempting to make contact, but there was no response. Around noon, a wild gust of wind roared in from the west, making us fear for our own camp's safety. Thankfully, it calmed down after a while, with only one last strong burst at two in the afternoon.

By three o'clock, everything was still, so we increased our efforts to reach Lake. Since his team had four planes, each with working short-wave radios, it didn't seem possible that a simple accident could have disabled all their communication equipment at once. But the silence remained. Thinking about how strong the wind must have been at his location, we started fearing the worst.

By six o'clock, our concern had turned into real alarm. After discussing the situation with Douglas and Thorfinnssen over the radio,

I decided we had to take action. The fifth plane, which we had left at the McMurdo Sound supply station with Sherman and two sailors, was in perfect condition and ready to fly at a moment's notice. It seemed like the exact kind of emergency we had saved it for.

I contacted Sherman and ordered him to fly the plane, along with the two sailors, Gunnarsson and Larsen, to our base as quickly as possible since the weather seemed favorable. Then we discussed who would be part of the search team. We decided to take everyone, along with the sled and dogs that I had kept with me. Even with such a large load, the plane—built specially for carrying heavy equipment—could handle it. Throughout this time, I kept trying to reach Lake over the radio, but there was still no response.

Sherman and the sailors took off at 7:30 p.m. and reported a smooth flight. They arrived at our base at midnight, and we immediately started planning our next move. Flying over Antarctica in a single plane, without any backup bases along the way, was extremely risky. But no one hesitated—it was clear we had no other choice.

We stayed up until 2:00 a.m., doing some initial loading of the plane, then took a short rest before getting up again four hours later to finish packing.

At 7:15 a.m. on January 25th, we took off, with McTighe as the pilot. Our team consisted of ten men, seven dogs, a sled, food, fuel, and other supplies, including the plane's wireless radio. The weather was clear, the air was calm, and the temperature was mild. We didn't expect any trouble reaching the coordinates Lake had given for his camp.

But what truly worried us wasn't the journey—it was what we might find, or not find, when we got there. The radio remained silent.

No matter how many calls we sent out, there was still no answer from Lake's team.

***

Every moment of that four-and-a-half-hour flight is burned into my memory because it changed my life forever. At fifty-four, I lost the sense of peace and certainty that most people have about the world and its natural laws. From that moment on, the ten of us—especially Danforth and me—would live with the terrible knowledge of things we could never forget. If we had the choice, we would never share what we saw with the rest of the world.

The newspapers printed our updates from the plane, describing our steady flight, two struggles with dangerous winds, and the sight of the broken ground where Lake had drilled his shaft three days earlier. We also reported seeing the strange rolling snow formations that Amundsen and Byrd had mentioned during their own explorations. But there came a point when words could no longer explain what we felt, and later, when we had to keep certain details secret.

The first person to spot the distant peaks was Larsen, one of the sailors. His shouts sent everyone rushing to the windows. Even though our plane was moving fast, the jagged, sharp-edged peaks seemed to rise painfully slowly, which meant they had to be unimaginably far away and incredibly tall.

Little by little, they grew larger on the horizon, revealing their dark, lifeless summits. Against the eerie glow of the Antarctic sky and the shifting clouds of icy dust, the sight filled us with a strange, dreamlike unease. There was something unsettling about those towering spires, as if they guarded the entrance to a forbidden and ancient world, filled with secrets beyond human understanding.

The glowing, swirling clouds behind the peaks gave an eerie impression of something vast and unknown—something beyond normal space and time. It was as if this place had been cut off from the rest of the world for countless ages, untouched, frozen, and forgotten. The feeling of isolation and mystery was overwhelming, and deep inside, I couldn't shake the sense that we were looking at something that should never have been seen.

***

It was young Danforth who first noticed the unusual shapes along the highest peaks of the mountains. They looked like pieces of perfectly shaped cubes, just as Lake had described in his messages. These formations reminded us of ancient, crumbling temples, similar to those seen in old paintings of misty mountain landscapes in Asia.

There was something unsettling about the entire landscape. It had an otherworldly feel, just like when we had first spotted Victoria Land back in October. Now, that feeling was even stronger. The eerie scene brought to mind old myths and legends, making me uneasy. This frozen, lifeless land seemed strangely similar to the legendary plateau of Leng, a place feared in ancient writings.

Mythologists believe Leng is in Central Asia, but human memory—and perhaps even the memory of beings before us—is long. It is possible that some of these stories have been passed down from places far older than Asia, from lands and creatures that existed before recorded history.

Some scholars have even suggested that the ancient Pnakotic Manuscripts were written before the Ice Age and that those who worshiped the strange being Tsathoggua were not human at all. Wherever Leng truly was—whether in space or time—I knew I never wanted to be near it. And standing in this desolate land, where Lake had just found unexplainable things, made me feel uncomfortably close to such horrors.

At that moment, I regretted ever reading the dreaded Necronomicon or spending so much time discussing strange folklore with Professor Wilmarth at the university. Some knowledge, I realized, is better left unknown.

***

As we neared the mountains and saw the rolling foothills ahead, a strange mirage appeared in the shimmering sky. I had seen many polar mirages before, some just as eerie and lifelike, but this one felt different—almost like a warning. As the swirling ice mist cleared, towering walls, spires, and strange, twisted buildings seemed to rise in the air above us.

The vision looked like a massive, ancient city, but not one built by humans. Its dark, towering structures seemed to defy normal rules of geometry. There were wide, sloping cones, tall cylinders with odd bulging tops, and stacks of flat, thin disks that formed jagged towers. Some of the shapes looked like overlapping five-pointed stars, while others were pyramids perched on top of cubes or stretched into impossibly high spires. Bridges of hollow tubes connected many of these structures, crisscrossing the sky at terrifying heights. The sheer size of it all felt overwhelming, as if it had been built for something far larger than humans.

The mirage reminded me of the wild sketches made by the Arctic explorer Scoresby in 1820, but this was far more unsettling. With the dark, unknown peaks towering ahead of us, thoughts of Lake's discovery in our minds, and the possibility of disaster weighing heavily on us, the sight filled me with an unshakable sense of dread. I was relieved when the illusion finally broke apart, though in its final moments, the shapes became even more monstrous before fading back into a shimmering haze.

We turned our attention back to the ground and saw that we were close to our destination. The massive mountains loomed ahead, their unnatural formations now clear even without a telescope. Below us, among the ice and rocky patches of the plateau, we spotted two dark shapes that appeared to be Lake's camp and drilling site. The tallest foothills were still several miles away, forming a separate range from the towering peaks that stretched beyond them.

Ropes, the student now piloting the plane, began to descend toward the larger dark spot, which seemed to be the camp. As he did, McTighe sent out the last uncensored radio message that the outside world would ever receive from our expedition.

Everyone has read the brief, incomplete news reports about the rest of our time in Antarctica. Hours after landing, we sent out a carefully worded message about the tragedy we found. We reluctantly reported that the entire Lake party had been wiped out, likely by the violent storm of the previous day or night. Eleven were confirmed dead. One, young Gedney, was missing.

People accepted our unclear explanation, knowing we must have been overwhelmed by what we saw. They believed us when we said the storm had damaged the bodies so badly that we couldn't take them with us. Even in our shock and fear, we had not lied. But the things we couldn't bring ourselves to say—the truth we are still afraid to speak of—are far more important. I am only sharing it now to warn others to stay away from these unknown horrors.

***

The storm had caused terrible destruction. Even without the other thing, it's uncertain if anyone could have survived. The violent winds, carrying sharp ice particles, were stronger than anything we had faced before. One of the plane shelters, which had been too weakly built, was nearly destroyed, and the derrick at the distant drilling site had been completely torn apart.

The metal parts of the planes and machinery were scratched and polished by the storm, and two of the smaller tents had been crushed despite being reinforced with snow. Any wooden surfaces left outside were stripped of paint, and all footprints in the snow had been completely erased.

None of the strange ancient specimens were intact enough to take back with us. However, we collected some minerals from a massive pile of debris, including a few of the odd greenish soapstone fragments with their five-pointed shapes and mysterious dot patterns. We also gathered some fossilized bones, including several that showed unusual injuries.

None of the dogs had survived. Their makeshift snow enclosure had been nearly destroyed—perhaps by the wind, though the way it was broken suggested the panicked animals may have tried to escape. All three sleds had disappeared, and we told ourselves the storm must have carried them off. The drilling equipment was too damaged to save, so we used it to seal off the eerie hole Lake had uncovered.

We left behind the two most damaged planes, as only four of us—Sherman, Danforth, McTighe, and Ropes—were skilled pilots, and Danforth was in no state to fly. We collected as many books, tools, and scientific instruments as we could, though much had been mysteriously blown away. Many of our extra tents and furs were either missing or unusable.

By 4 p.m., after searching by air and giving up hope of finding Gedney, we sent a cautious message to the Arkham for relaying. We kept the report calm and vague. The only sign of distress we mentioned was how the dogs had reacted fearfully to the biological specimens—something we expected from Lake's earlier descriptions. However, we didn't say that the dogs had also reacted the same way to the strange soapstone pieces and other disturbed objects, including parts of our equipment that seemed to have been moved or tampered with by a force more curious than any natural wind.

About the fourteen specimens, we were deliberately unclear. We said the ones we found were too damaged to take back but that they matched Lake's descriptions exactly. It was difficult to keep our emotions out of it, and we avoided giving details on how we found them. We had already agreed not to say anything that might suggest Lake's team had gone mad. After all, how would it sound to say that we found six of the imperfect specimens carefully buried in nine-foot snow graves, each marked by five-pointed mounds covered in the same strange dot patterns as the soapstone artifacts? The eight perfect specimens Lake had described had completely vanished.

We also chose not to tell the full truth about our terrifying trip over the mountains the next day. Only a plane carrying the bare minimum weight could clear such heights, so it had to be just the two of us— Danforth and me. When we returned at 1 a.m., Danforth was barely holding himself together. He was close to losing his mind but managed to stay quiet. It didn't take much convincing to get him to agree not to share our sketches, or mention what we found, beyond what we had decided to report. We even hid our camera film to develop later in secret. What I am about to tell now will be as new to the rest of our crew as it is to the outside world. In fact, Danforth has stayed more silent than I have—because he saw, or thinks he saw, something even he refuses to talk about.

Our official report spoke only of a difficult climb and confirmed Lake's belief that the mountains were made of ancient slate, unchanged for millions of years. We noted the unusual cube-like formations, suggested that the cave openings were formed by dissolved limestone, and speculated that experienced climbers could eventually find a way to cross the entire range. We also reported that the other side of the mountains held a massive plateau, just as ancient as the peaks themselves—20,000 feet high, covered in thin ice, with strange rock formations poking through the surface.

Everything we said was technically true, and our team accepted it without question. We claimed our sixteen-hour absence—much longer than expected—was due to strong winds, though we admitted to landing briefly on the other side. Our explanation sounded ordinary enough that no one was tempted to follow us. If anyone had tried, I would have done everything I could to stop them. I don't even know how Danforth would have reacted.

While we were gone, Pabodie, Sherman, Ropes, McTighe, and Williamson had worked hard to repair Lake's two best planes, though the way the machines had been strangely taken apart and moved around remained unexplained.

The next morning, we planned to load everything onto the planes and leave. The safest route back was to return to our old base before heading toward McMurdo Sound. Flying straight across the unknown parts of this dead continent was too risky. After all that had happened—after the tragedies, the destruction of our equipment, and the horrors we still could not speak of—none of us had any desire to stay in this land of cold, emptiness, and madness. We just wanted to escape.

***

As everyone knows, we returned safely without any further trouble. By the evening of January 27th, all our planes had arrived back at the old base after a quick, nonstop flight. The next day, January 28th, we flew to McMurdo Sound in two stages, pausing briefly to fix a rudder issue caused by the strong winds over the ice shelf after we had crossed the vast plateau.

Five days later, the Arkham and Miskatonic, with all of us and our equipment aboard, broke free from the thickening ice and sailed through Ross Sea. Behind us, the eerie mountains of Victoria Land loomed against the stormy sky, their peaks twisting the howling wind into strange, ghostly sounds that sent a deep chill through me.

Less than two weeks after that, we had left all signs of the polar land behind us. I silently thanked whatever forces existed that we had escaped that cursed place—a land where life and death, time and space, had formed dark, unnatural connections since the beginning of the world.

Since returning, we have done everything possible to discourage further expeditions to Antarctica. We have kept many of our fears and theories to ourselves, staying silent out of loyalty to each other and for the good of the world. Even Danforth, who suffered a nervous breakdown, has never lost control and revealed what we swore to hide.

There is one thing, however, that Danforth believes only he saw—something so terrible that he refuses to tell even me. I think speaking about it might help him recover, but whenever he comes close to revealing it in moments of weakness, he quickly takes it back, as if even admitting it to himself is too much to bear. I sometimes wonder if it was just his mind playing tricks on him after all we had been through.

It will not be easy to stop others from exploring the frozen south. In fact, our efforts may have the opposite effect, drawing more attention instead. We should have known that human curiosity never fades, and that the discoveries we reported would only push others to continue the search for the unknown.

Lake's reports about those ancient life forms have excited scientists, especially biologists and paleontologists. However, we were careful not to show them the body parts we took from the buried specimens or the photographs of how we found them. We also kept hidden the strange, damaged bones and the eerie green soapstone fragments. Danforth and I have been especially cautious with the sketches and photographs we made on the massive plateau beyond the mountains, as well as the things we found there—the things we studied in horror before tucking them away in our pockets.

But now, the Starkweather-Moore expedition is preparing to go back, and they are far better equipped than we ever were. If they are not stopped, they will reach the heart of Antarctica. They will drill and dig until they unearth something we know should stay buried— something that could bring about the end of the world.

Now, at last, I have to speak. Even about the ultimate, indescribable terror that waits beyond the mountains of madness.

Chapter IV

I can barely bring myself to think about what we really found at Lake's camp—or the even worse thing beyond the towering mountains.

I've already described the destruction caused by the wind, the damaged shelters, the scattered equipment, the strange behavior of the dogs, the missing sleds, and the loss of men and animals. I also mentioned the strange way six of Lake's specimens were buried, their bodies oddly well-preserved despite their injuries. But I don't remember if I said that, when counting the dead dogs, we found one missing. At the time, we didn't think much of it. Only Danforth and I have really considered what it could mean.

What I have held back concerns the bodies—and some disturbing details that might give a terrible meaning to the chaos we found. I tried to distract the men from these things because it was easier, and far less terrifying, to blame everything on madness. The wind alone, screaming through that desolate, mysterious place, could have been enough to drive someone insane.

But the worst part, of course, was what had happened to the bodies—both men and dogs. They had been violently attacked, torn apart in horrifying ways that made no sense. As far as we could tell, they had died from strangulation or deep wounds.

It seemed the dogs had started the panic. Their enclosure had been broken from the inside, as if they had tried to escape in a frenzy. The camp had placed them far away from the strange specimens they feared, but that hadn't been enough. Maybe the wind itself had terrified them, or perhaps those ancient remains had begun to give off some odor that drove them wild. Whatever happened, it had been brutal.

Now, I must put aside hesitation and tell the worst of it—though I will be clear that Danforth and I both agreed that Gedney, who was missing, was not responsible for what we found.

I already said the bodies were badly damaged, but now I must add that some had been cut apart in a methodical, almost surgical way. Both men and dogs had been treated the same. The healthiest bodies had been carefully carved up, with large sections of tissue removed, as if by an experienced butcher. To make things even more unsettling, a strange amount of salt—taken from the food stores—had been sprinkled around them. The idea of what this suggested was almost too horrible to think about.

The worst of it had happened inside a broken-down airplane shelter. The plane itself had been dragged out, and the winds had erased any tracks that might have explained what had happened. Torn pieces of clothing lay scattered around, but they gave no clues.

Even stranger, in a protected corner of the shelter, we found faint tracks in the snow—but they weren't human. They looked eerily similar to the fossilized prints Lake had been studying. In this place, under these looming, unnatural mountains, we had to be very careful about letting our imaginations run wild.

In the end, Gedney and one dog were still missing. At first, we thought two men had disappeared, but when we checked the dissection tent, we found something gruesome.

The remains of one man and one dog had been taken apart inside the tent. The pieces had been carefully, though clumsily, dissected, as if someone—or something—had been trying to study them. I will not name the man, for the sake of any family he left behind.

Lake's surgical tools were missing, but they had clearly been used and then cleaned with care. The camp's gasoline stove was also gone, though we found spent matches scattered around it. We buried what was left of the man with the others, and the dog's remains with the rest of the animals.

There were other mysteries, too. The missing sleds, the lost biological specimens, and the disappearance of supplies like food, fuel, books, and tools made no sense. Some of the scientific instruments and machines had been strangely tampered with, as if someone unfamiliar with them had tried to examine or use them. Even the dogs reacted with fear toward the disturbed equipment.

The food supply had been raided, but in bizarre ways. Some cans had been opened in places where no person would have thought to do so. There were scattered matches everywhere, some whole, some broken, some burned. Tent cloths and fur suits had been sliced apart in strange ways, as if someone had tried to alter them for an impossible use.

The brutal treatment of the bodies and the unnatural way the specimens had been buried all pointed to something deeply unsettling. We took as many photographs as we could, knowing that one day we might need to use them to stop others from making the same mistake we had.

With these pictures, we will try to prevent the Starkweather-Moore Expedition from venturing into this cursed place.

***

The first thing we did after discovering the bodies in the shelter was take photographs and dig up the unusual graves marked by five-pointed snow mounds. We couldn't help but notice how these eerie mounds, with their groups of small dots, looked just like the strange greenish soapstones Lake had described. When we later found some of those soapstones mixed in with the minerals, the resemblance was impossible to ignore.

The whole scene reminded us of the star-shaped heads of the ancient creatures Lake had discovered. We agreed that this resemblance must have deeply affected Lake's team, already pushed to their mental limits.

Everyone openly accepted the idea that Gedney, if he had survived, had lost his mind and caused all of this. No one voiced any other theories, though I am sure each of us had thoughts too disturbing to say out loud.

That afternoon, Sherman, Pabodie, and McTighe flew over the area, searching with binoculars for Gedney or any missing equipment. They found nothing. The massive mountain range stretched endlessly in both directions, just as high and imposing no matter where they looked. On some peaks, the cube-like formations were even clearer, looking even more like the ancient ruins in those eerie paintings of Asian mountains. The dark openings of caves were scattered all along the bare summits.

Despite our fear, we couldn't help but feel the pull of curiosity. What lay beyond those mountains?

That night, after everything we had seen, we forced ourselves to rest, but we had already decided on our next move. The next morning, we would take a small plane over the mountains with a camera and geology tools. Danforth and I would go first.

We woke at seven a.m., ready for an early start, but strong winds delayed us until nearly nine.

I have already told the version of events we shared with the men at camp and later reported to the outside world. But now I must tell the truth—the full story of what we really saw beyond those mountains. It was these discoveries that eventually broke Danforth's mind.

Even now, I wish he would speak about the thing he believes only he saw. I think it was just his mind playing tricks on him, a final shock that pushed him over the edge. But he refuses to discuss it. All I have are his broken whispers, muttered when he is barely in control of himself.

If what I reveal is not enough to keep others away from the heart of Antarctica—if they continue to dig into this forbidden, lifeless wasteland—then whatever horrors follow will not be my fault.

Danforth and I studied Pabodie's notes from his flight the day before. Using a sextant, we determined that the lowest mountain pass in sight of our camp was around twenty-three or twenty-four thousand feet above sea level. Our camp itself was already at twelve thousand feet, so we wouldn't have to climb as high as it seemed.

Still, we could feel the thin air and freezing cold as we ascended. We had to leave the cabin windows open for visibility, and despite our heavy furs, we shivered as we approached the jagged, ominous peaks.

As we neared, we saw more of the strange, regular shapes clinging to the mountainsides—shapes that reminded us again of those mysterious paintings of ancient ruins.

Lake's reports had been right. The rock layers showed that these peaks had remained unchanged for tens of millions of years—perhaps even longer. We could only guess how much taller they had once been.

Something about this region seemed to resist the natural processes of erosion, keeping these mountains preserved in their terrible, unnatural state.

But it wasn't the mountains themselves that disturbed us the most. It was the maze of cube-shaped structures, walls, and cave openings scattered across them. I examined them with binoculars and took aerial photographs while Danforth piloted the plane. At times, we switched places so he could study them too.

Many of the formations were made of a light-colored, ancient quartzite that didn't match any rock we had seen elsewhere in the region. Their geometric precision was disturbing, more extreme than anything Lake had described.

Though weathering had worn down their edges over the ages, they remained eerily solid. The sight reminded us of the ruins of Machu Picchu or the oldest foundation walls unearthed in ancient Mesopotamian cities. Like Lake and his team before us, we sometimes got the strange impression that these were separate, enormous blocks stacked together.

I could not explain what we were seeing. As a geologist, I felt completely at a loss. Some natural rock formations, like the famous Giant's Causeway in Ireland, could have strange, regular shapes. But this mountain range was clearly not volcanic, despite Lake's early theories.

Then there were the cave openings. They were oddly symmetrical, almost perfectly square or semicircular, as if something had shaped them long ago. Their numbers and placement suggested an extensive tunnel network running through the mountains.

We couldn't see far inside, but from what little we glimpsed, they seemed free of stalactites and stalagmites. The ground around the openings was strangely smooth, as if worn down over time.

Danforth, still haunted by what we had found at the camp, suggested something that made my skin crawl. He said the cracks and marks near the cave mouths reminded him of the strange dot patterns on the ancient greenish soapstones—the same markings that had been eerily copied onto the snow graves.

***

We continued to climb as we flew over the higher foothills, heading toward the relatively low mountain pass we had chosen. As we moved forward, we occasionally glanced down at the snow and ice below, wondering if we could have made the journey using the basic equipment of earlier explorers.

To our surprise, the terrain didn't seem as difficult as we had expected. Despite some dangerous crevasses and rough patches, it looked like something that explorers like Scott, Shackleton, or Amundsen could have managed with their sledges. Some of the glaciers appeared to lead smoothly up to wind-swept passes, and when we reached the one we had selected, we found it was no different.

The feeling of anticipation as we neared the top, preparing to look out over an untouched world, is difficult to describe. Even though we had no reason to think the land beyond the mountains would be much different from what we had already seen, there was something strange about this place. The towering peaks had an eerie presence, and the shimmering sky between them seemed to whisper of secrets best left unknown. It was a feeling not easily put into words—more of a deep, unsettling impression tied to strange myths, forgotten stories, and the kind of eerie beauty found in old paintings and poetry.

Even the wind sounded unnatural. As it howled through the caves in the cliffs, there was an odd whistling, almost like a distant melody. For a brief moment, I thought I heard something strange in the wind—something unsettling, like a faint and twisted echo of something familiar yet completely out of place.

At last, after a slow and steady climb, we reached an altitude of 23,570 feet. Below us, the clinging snow had disappeared, leaving behind only dark, bare rock slopes and jagged glaciers. But among these desolate cliffs, we could still see those unnatural cube-like structures, towering walls, and deep, shadowy cave mouths—things that looked out of place in this frozen wilderness.

Looking along the mountain range, I thought I spotted the peak Lake had described—the one with a strange wall built right on top. It was half-hidden by an odd haze, similar to the one that had once made Lake believe the area might have volcanic activity.

The pass stretched before us, smooth and swept clean by the wind, framed by sharp, looming cliffs that seemed almost alive in their ominous stillness. Beyond it, swirling mist and the dim glow of the low polar sun lit the sky of an unknown land—a place no human had ever seen.

A few more feet of altitude, and we would witness it for ourselves. Danforth and I, unable to speak over the roar of the engines and the howling wind, exchanged a tense glance. Then, as we rose those last few feet, we finally saw what lay beyond—an ancient and utterly alien world, untouched by time.

Chapter V

I think both of us shouted at the same time, overwhelmed by a mix of awe, fear, wonder, and disbelief as we cleared the pass and saw what lay beyond. At first, we must have tried to explain it in a way that made sense. Maybe we compared it to the strange rock formations of the Garden of the Gods in Colorado or the oddly shaped, wind-carved stones of the Arizona desert. Perhaps, for a moment, we even thought it was another mirage, like the one we had seen the day before as we approached these eerie mountains.

We had to cling to some logical explanation as our eyes took in the vast, storm-battered plateau stretching before us. It was covered in an endless maze of towering, carefully arranged stone structures. Their massive forms rose above the ice, their surfaces worn and cracked, yet still strangely symmetrical. The glacial layer covering the ground was only about forty or fifty feet deep at most, and in some places, it was even thinner.

The sight was beyond words. It was as if the natural order of the world had been broken. This was a place that should not exist—an ancient land, twenty thousand feet above sea level, in a climate that had been too harsh for life for at least half a million years. And yet, as far as we could see, there stretched a network of massive, structured stone formations. No force of nature could have shaped them so perfectly. No random erosion or shifting ice could have created such precise patterns. The only possible explanation—one we struggled to accept—was that they had been built.

***

The sight before us was impossible to describe! It felt like a terrible break in the natural order of the world!

***

We had never seriously believed that the strange cubes and walls on the mountainsides were anything but natural formations. After all, how could they be anything else when humans were barely different from apes at the time this frozen land became locked in ice?

But now, our sense of reason was shaken. The massive maze of shaped stone blocks—some squared, some curved, some angled—had details that made it impossible to dismiss. It was, without a doubt, the same nightmarish city we had glimpsed in the mirage, but now it was real, solid, and inescapable. That eerie vision had not been a trick of the light—it had reflected an actual place across the mountains. The ice and air must have created an illusion, stretching and distorting its image, but standing before the real thing, we found it even more terrifying than its ghostly reflection.

***

It was, very clearly, the blasphemous city of the mirage—in stark, objective reality!

***

Only the immense, unnatural size of these towering stone structures had kept them from being completely destroyed over hundreds of thousands—maybe even millions—of years. They had stood through endless storms on this frozen, desolate plateau. "Corona Mundi—Roof of the World—" Strange phrases filled our minds as we stared down in disbelief at the impossible sight before us.

Once again, I couldn't shake the eerie ancient legends that had haunted me ever since we first arrived in this lifeless Antarctic world. I thought of the cursed plateau of Leng, the terrifying Mi-Go or

Abominable Snow Men of the Himalayas, the Pnakotic Manuscripts filled with stories of beings older than humanity, the dark Cthulhu cult, the forbidden Necronomicon, and the chilling Hyperborean myths of the formless Tsathoggua and the even more dreadful creatures said to be connected to it.

***

The strange ruins stretched endlessly in all directions, showing no sign of thinning except for a small break near the pass we had just flown through. It became clear that we had stumbled upon only a small section of something much larger than we could imagine.

The foothills had fewer of the eerie stone structures, but they still connected the ruined city to the cube-like outposts along the mountainsides. These outer buildings, along with the dark cave openings, were just as thick on the inner side of the mountains as they were on the outer side.

The massive stone maze was mostly made up of towering walls, some as high as 150 feet, and many between five and ten feet thick. Most of the structures were built from huge blocks of ancient rock—dark slate, schist, and sandstone. Some blocks were as large as $4 \times 6 \times 8$ feet, while other sections seemed to be carved directly from the bedrock.

The buildings varied in size and shape, with some resembling giant honeycombs stretching across great distances, while others stood alone. Many were shaped like cones, pyramids, or terraces, though we also saw perfect cylinders, cubes, clusters of cubes, and even some with five-sided layouts that reminded us of modern fortresses. The use of arches was clear, and we believed domes had once existed before time wore them away.

The entire city was battered and weathered, its crumbling walls surrounded by fallen stone blocks and ancient debris. In some areas, the glaciers were clear enough for us to see the lower parts of the towers, along with preserved stone bridges that once connected them at different heights. Many of these bridges had collapsed over time, leaving only scars where they had once been.

Looking closer, we saw many large windows, some still sealed with what seemed to be ancient wooden shutters turned to stone. Others gaped open, adding to the eerie, lifeless feel of the place. Some buildings had lost their roofs, leaving jagged edges that had been smoothed by the relentless wind, while others still held their original shape, protected by surrounding structures. With our field glasses, we spotted horizontal carvings along some of the walls, including the strange dot patterns that matched those found on the green soapstones, now taking on a greater, more chilling significance.

Many areas had collapsed completely, leaving deep cracks in the ice. In other spots, the stonework had been worn down to the level of the glacier itself. One particular stretch, leading from the plateau's interior to a gap in the foothills, was entirely free of buildings. We guessed this had once been the path of a massive river millions of years ago, flowing through the city before vanishing into an underground abyss beneath the towering mountains. This place, above all else, seemed to be filled with endless caves, hidden depths, and mysteries beyond human understanding.

Looking back, I can barely comprehend how we kept our composure while flying over this impossible ruin. We knew something was terribly wrong—whether it was the timeline of history, scientific theories, or even our own perception of reality. But we remained focused enough to control the plane, take detailed observations, and capture photographs that might one day prove useful.

For me, my lifelong training as a scientist may have kept me grounded. Even through the fear and confusion, my curiosity burned stronger than ever. I wanted—needed—to understand what kind of beings had built this enormous city and how they fit into the history of the world.

This was no ordinary city. It had to be the heart of some forgotten and incredible chapter of Earth's past, a civilization lost so long ago that only the most obscure and twisted myths had faintly remembered it.

Here lay an ancient metropolis beyond anything known to history, dwarfing legends like Atlantis and Lemuria. It stood among the whispered horrors of lost civilizations—Valusia, R'lyeh, Ib of the land of Mnar, and the Nameless City buried deep in the Arabian desert.

As we flew over those towering ruins, my mind ran wild, making connections between this forsaken place and my own nightmares of the horrors at the camp.

We had only partially filled the plane's fuel tank to make it lighter, so we had to be careful with how much ground we covered. Even so, we explored an enormous area, flying low enough to avoid the worst of the wind.

The mountain range and the terrifying ruins at its base seemed to stretch endlessly. After flying fifty miles in each direction, we saw no end to the vast maze of stone structures rising like the dead from beneath the ice.

Still, there were some strange variations. One of the most fascinating was a canyon where the ancient river had once flowed through the foothills, its path marked with mysterious carvings that hinted at secrets lost to time.

The entrance to the river had massive stone pillars carved into strange shapes, and both Danforth and I felt an eerie sense of familiarity, as if we had seen these ridged, barrel-like patterns before in some forgotten nightmare.

As we flew over the ruins, we noticed several large, star-shaped open spaces that looked like public squares, along with hills that had been hollowed out into sprawling stone structures. However, two hills stood out—one was so eroded that we couldn't tell what had once been there, while the other still had a towering monument carved from solid rock. Its strange conical shape reminded us of the ancient Snake Tomb in Petra.

Moving further inland from the mountains, we realized that while the city stretched endlessly along the foothills, it wasn't infinitely wide. After about thirty miles, the dense stone buildings started to thin out, and ten miles beyond that, the land became an empty wasteland with no sign of structures. A wide, sunken path marked where the river had once flowed beyond the city, while the landscape became more rugged, sloping gently upward into the misty horizon.

We hadn't landed yet, but leaving this strange place without stepping inside one of the massive ruins seemed unthinkable. We decided to land near the foothills, close to the pass we would use for our return trip. From the air, we spotted several flat areas suitable for landing, and by 12:30 p.m., we safely touched down on a hard, snow-covered plain, free of obstacles and well-suited for takeoff when the time came.

Since we didn't plan to stay long and the winds at this altitude were calm, we didn't bother building a snow barrier around the plane.

Instead, we made sure the skis were securely set and that the plane's essential parts were protected from the cold.

For our short exploration, we left behind our heaviest flying gear and packed only what we needed: a pocket compass, hand camera, small food supply, notebooks, a geologist's hammer and chisel, specimen bags, climbing rope, and electric torches with extra batteries. We had brought this equipment in case we found a good place to land and collect rock samples, take ground photos, or map out the area.

We also had extra paper, which we tore into small pieces and placed in a bag. If we found ourselves in a maze of tunnels, we could drop pieces along the way to mark our path instead of using the slower method of carving rock markings.

Walking carefully down the snow-covered slope toward the towering ruins ahead, we felt the same sense of overwhelming discovery that had filled us when approaching the unknown mountain pass earlier that morning. Even though we had already seen this impossible city from the air, the idea of actually stepping inside buildings that had been constructed by unknown beings millions of years ago was both thrilling and deeply unsettling.

Despite the thin air at this extreme altitude, we both felt strong enough to push forward, determined to uncover whatever secrets this ancient place held.

Within moments, we reached a ruined structure that had been worn down to the level of the snow. Just ten or fifteen paces beyond that, we saw a massive five-pointed wall, still standing without a roof, towering about ten or eleven feet high. We made our way toward it, and when we finally placed our hands on its weathered stone blocks, we felt as if we had broken into a time long forgotten—one that should have remained untouched by human hands.

This star-shaped structure stretched nearly three hundred feet across and was built from enormous sandstone blocks, each about six by eight feet. Along its outer walls, we saw a series of arched openings—possibly windows—each around four feet wide and five feet tall, evenly spaced along the star's points and inner angles. The openings were about four feet above the frozen ground.

Peering through them, we could see that the walls were at least five feet thick, with no inner partitions remaining. Faint carvings or bas-reliefs lined the interior walls, just as we had suspected when flying over similar ruins. Though the structure likely had lower sections long ago, they were now buried deep beneath ice and snow, leaving only this towering remnant of an ancient world.

We climbed through one of the windows and tried to make sense of the faded wall carvings, but they were too worn to understand. We didn't disturb the thick ice covering the floor, knowing from our flights that other buildings in the city were less buried. Some still had intact roofs, and we hoped they might have open spaces leading down to the original ground level.

Before leaving the wall, we took careful photographs and studied its massive stonework, still puzzled by how such enormous blocks had been placed without mortar. We wished Pabodie was with us—his engineering knowledge might have helped explain how this ancient city had been built so long ago.

The half-mile walk downhill toward the city, with the wind howling fiercely through the towering peaks behind us, was something I will never forget. The strange, dark towers ahead shifted into new shapes at every step, their bizarre angles and unnatural forms looking like something from a dream. If we hadn't taken photographs, I might have doubted whether such a place truly existed.

The stonework of the buildings matched what we had seen in the wall, but the shapes here were even stranger—beyond anything words could describe. There were twisted, irregular cones, uneven terraces, thick columns with bulging tops, broken pillars arranged in eerie patterns, and countless five-pointed formations that made no sense.

As we got closer, we could see through the clear sections of ice, spotting stone bridges that connected different buildings at different heights. There seemed to be no proper streets, just a chaotic maze of passageways. The only wide, open space was about a mile to the left, likely the path of an ancient river that had once flowed through the city and into the mountains.

Looking through our field glasses, we saw many faded carvings on the outer walls, along with the strange dot clusters that had first appeared on the green soapstones. We could only imagine what the city once looked like when it was whole, its towers still standing tall. From above, it must have been a tangled web of twisting alleys, with some streets nearly enclosed by overhanging walls and bridges.

The ruins stretched out before us like something from a dream, fading into the misty western horizon. The low Antarctic sun, shining weakly through the haze, cast an eerie reddish glow over the scene. When a thicker cloud briefly blocked the light, the city suddenly felt even more menacing, as if something unnatural still lurked in its depths. Even the wind, whispering through the mountain caves behind us, seemed to take on a more sinister tone.

The last stretch of our descent was steep, forcing us to climb down carefully. A section of rock at the edge of the slope made us suspect that a man-made terrace had once stood there. We guessed that beneath the ice, there might still be a hidden staircase leading into the city.

Once we finally stepped inside the ruins, climbing over fallen stone and feeling dwarfed by the towering, crumbling walls, our sense of unease only grew. The place felt oppressive, as if it had been waiting for us for ages. Danforth became noticeably uneasy, making nervous, off-topic remarks about the horror at the camp. I was irritated by his words, yet deep down, I couldn't ignore the same disturbing thoughts creeping into my mind.

The strange atmosphere affected Danforth more than he wanted to admit. At one point, as we turned a corner filled with rubble, he claimed to see faint markings on the ground that disturbed him. Later, he stopped abruptly, saying he heard a muffled musical sound—like the wind in the mountain caves, but somehow different in a way he couldn't explain.

The constant presence of five-pointed shapes—on the buildings, in the carvings, and even in the layout of the city—felt like an unspoken message from the past. We both sensed, without saying it, that this place had once been home to something ancient and beyond human understanding.

Even with the overwhelming sense of unease, our curiosity as scientists kept us moving forward. We gathered samples of the different types of rock used in the buildings, hoping they might reveal the true age of the city. None of the outer walls contained anything newer than the Jurassic or Comanchean periods, and no stone in the entire place seemed younger than the Pliocene age.

It was a chilling realization—we were walking through ruins that had been abandoned for at least five hundred thousand years. Possibly even longer.

***

As we moved through the maze of towering stone walls, we stopped at every possible opening to look inside and find ways to enter. Some were too high to reach, while others led only to ice-filled ruins as empty as the wall we had explored earlier.

One large opening looked promising, but when we peered inside, we saw only a dark, bottomless pit with no visible way down. Occasionally, we found the remains of wooden shutters, now petrified with age. The grain of the wood was still visible, proving that it had come from ancient trees—some as old as the Cretaceous period. We found nothing more recent than the Pliocene era.

The placement of the shutters was inconsistent—some were on the inside of the windows, while others were on the outside. The edges showed signs of old hinges, now long gone, suggesting they had once been fixed in place with metal. Over time, they had wedged themselves into position, staying intact despite the loss of their original fasteners.

Eventually, we came across a row of windows in the curved walls of a massive five-sided cone, which appeared well preserved. Inside, we could see a huge open chamber with a stone floor, likely some sort of hall. However, the windows were too high for us to climb down without using a rope. We had brought one, but we weren't eager to use it unless absolutely necessary—especially in the thin air at this high altitude, which made physical effort more exhausting.

Our flashlights revealed bold carvings along the walls of this vast chamber, arranged in wide bands separated by decorative designs. We made a note of its location, intending to enter later unless we found an easier way into another building.

Finally, we discovered exactly what we needed—an archway about six feet wide and ten feet high. It had once been part of a bridge that spanned a narrow alley, now buried under ice about five feet below.

Because the building's upper floor still existed, we could step right in without having to climb.

The structure on our side of the alley was a rectangular series of terraces facing west. Across from it stood a worn-down cylindrical tower with no windows and a strange bulge about ten feet above the entrance. Its interior was completely dark, and the archway seemed to open into an endless pit.

A pile of rubble made it easy to enter the larger building, but we hesitated for a moment. Even though we had already made our way into this ancient and mysterious city, stepping inside a fully intact building—one that had been standing for unimaginable ages—felt like a moment of no return. Everything we had seen so far made the truth about this place increasingly clear and deeply unsettling.

Still, we forced ourselves forward, climbing through the opening. Inside, the floor was made of large slate slabs, leading into a long, high corridor with walls covered in carvings.

Seeing many inner doorways branching off in different directions, we realized just how complicated this network of rooms and passages could be. Up until now, we had relied on our compasses and the sight of the mountains behind us to keep from getting lost, but we knew that wouldn't be enough anymore.

To keep track of our path, we tore extra paper into small pieces and placed them in a bag for Danforth to carry. We planned to drop these pieces along the way like a trail, a simple method that would help us find our way back—so long as no air currents disturbed them. If the paper proved unreliable, we could resort to chipping marks into the stone walls, though that would slow us down significantly.

There was no way to know just how far this underground world stretched. The way many of the buildings were connected suggested we might be able to move between them beneath the ice, except where collapses or rock formations blocked the way. Surprisingly, most of the rooms seemed untouched by ice, as if the structures had been sealed off before the glaciers formed.

Through the clear ice covering many of the windows, we saw that nearly all had been tightly shut with their ancient shutters, as if the entire city had been locked away before the cold took over. It almost seemed as if this place had been deliberately abandoned long ago rather than destroyed by some disaster.

Had the people who built it known the ice was coming? Had they left in time, searching for a new home somewhere else?

The exact details of how the ice sheet had formed here would have to wait for further study. Clearly, it had not been the result of slow, crushing pressure. Perhaps deep snowfall had accumulated over time, or maybe a great flood—caused by a broken glacial dam in the nearby mountains—had frozen solid, creating the eerie landscape we now explored.

In a place like this, the imagination could run wild.

Chapter VI

Describing our journey through that ancient, maze-like city in full detail would take too long. The place was a vast, empty ruin, untouched by any living thing for countless ages. It was filled with secrets from a time long before humans existed, and our footsteps echoed through its silent halls for the first time in millions of years.

Much of what we discovered came from studying the countless carvings on the walls. Our flashlight photographs will serve as proof of what we saw, though we regretted not bringing more film. Once we ran out, we had to make rough sketches in our notebooks of the most important details.

The building we entered was massive and complex, giving us a strong impression of the ancient civilization that built it. The outer walls were thick and solid, but inside, the rooms were slightly less massive, especially on the lower levels. The layout was an irregular maze, with floors at different heights, making navigation difficult. If not for the trail of torn paper we left behind, we would have been lost almost immediately.

We decided to start by exploring the upper levels, where parts of the building were crumbling and open to the sky. Climbing about a hundred feet, we reached the top tier of rooms, which were filled with snow and exposed to the freezing air. There were no stairs—only steep stone ramps with ridges that allowed us to climb.

The rooms came in all shapes and sizes, including five-pointed stars, triangles, and perfect cubes. Most were around 30 feet wide and 20 feet tall, though some were much larger. After carefully searching these upper sections and those at ground level, we moved downward, floor by floor, into the buried parts of the structure.

There, we quickly realized we were in a vast underground network of connected chambers and hallways, stretching far beyond this one building. The sheer size and weight of the stonework became overwhelming, and everything about the place felt deeply unnatural. The strange shapes, the proportions, and the way the walls were built all seemed designed for beings very different from humans.

By studying the carvings, we confirmed what we already suspected—the city was millions of years old. We still couldn't figure out how the builders had balanced such enormous blocks of stone, though it was clear they often relied on arches for support. The rooms were completely empty, further proving to us that the city had been abandoned on purpose rather than destroyed by some disaster.

The walls were covered in detailed carvings, arranged in wide horizontal bands, alternating between pictorial scenes and decorative geometric patterns. Occasionally, we saw smooth sections with small groups of dots—perhaps some form of writing.

The artistry of the carvings was beyond anything we had ever seen. The level of skill and precision was extraordinary, yet the style was completely different from any human culture. The smallest details of plants and animals were incredibly lifelike, even when carved on a grand scale. The geometric designs followed strict mathematical rules, with many based on the number five.

The artwork used a unique perspective, blending cross-sections with two-dimensional silhouettes, creating a strangely analytical effect. The closest comparison we could make was to the wildest works of modern artists, though even those were far less refined.

The carvings were made with deep, sharp lines. The background of the pictorial scenes was carved about two inches into the stone, while the decorative dot patterns were set slightly deeper. Some walls showed faint traces of color, suggesting that these images had once been painted, though time had erased most of the pigment.

The more we studied the carvings, the more we admired them. Despite their abstract style, they captured the true essence of every object. There was also something about them that felt just beyond our understanding, as if they contained hidden meanings or symbols that another species—perhaps the very beings that built this city—would have instantly recognized.

The images on the walls seemed to tell stories from the time these beings had lived here. Their deep focus on history turned out to be incredibly lucky for us. Because of this, the carvings provided more information than we ever could have hoped for, making their documentation our highest priority.

Some rooms looked different because they had large maps, star charts, and other scientific drawings. These images only confirmed what we had already learned from the carved walls and decorations, making everything even more disturbing.

I can only hope that telling this story won't make anyone too curious. If someone actually believes me, I want them to be cautious, not tempted to explore this place. It would be a terrible mistake if my warning had the opposite effect, leading people into danger.

The walls had tall windows and enormous twelve-foot doorways. Sometimes, we found the remains of ancient wooden doors and shutters—beautifully carved and polished, but now hardened into stone. All the metal parts had disappeared long ago, but a few doors were still standing. We had to push them aside to move from one room to another.

Some windows still had strange, slightly see-through glass, usually in an oval shape, though there weren't many left. We also saw large empty spaces in the walls, probably once used for storage or display. Sometimes, we found odd green soapstone statues in these spaces—either broken or simply left behind because they weren't considered valuable.

Other openings in the walls seemed to be part of an old mechanical system for heating and lighting, which we could guess from the carvings. The ceilings were usually plain, though some had fallen green soapstone tiles. The floors were mostly stone, but some had once been tiled as well.

As I mentioned before, there was no furniture left, but the wall carvings showed us what had once been here. The upper rooms were filled with dust, rubble, and broken pieces of stone. However, as we went deeper, we noticed that some rooms were much cleaner—just covered in a fine layer of dust or mineral deposits. In certain places, it even looked like someone had recently swept the floors, which was unsettling.

A central courtyard, which we had seen from above, let in enough light so that we didn't always need our flashlights on the upper floors. However, deeper inside, under the ice, the darkness grew thicker. Some areas at ground level were nearly pitch black.

It's hard to describe how we felt as we wandered through this enormous, ancient, abandoned city. It was more than just the crushing weight of its age and emptiness—there was also the horror of what had recently happened at our camp, and the terrifying images carved into the walls.

Then, we found a perfect section of carvings, one we could understand without any doubt. It only took a few moments of studying it to confirm the terrible truth—something Danforth and I had already suspected but had avoided saying out loud. There was no way to deny it anymore.

The creatures that had built and lived in this city had existed millions of years ago, long before humans evolved. Back then, our distant ancestors were just primitive mammals, and huge dinosaurs still roamed the lands of Europe and Asia.

Until now, we had clung to one last hope—that the five-pointed star symbol we kept seeing was only a cultural or religious decoration. Many ancient civilizations, like the Minoans in Crete, used symbols of animals they worshipped—the bull, the scarab beetle, the wolf, or the eagle. We had tried to convince ourselves that this was the same.

But now, that hope was gone. We had to face the horrifying reality that we had both secretly feared all along. I can barely bring myself to write it down, but by now, I think any reader has already figured it out.

***

The creatures that once lived in this terrifying city during the age of dinosaurs were not dinosaurs themselves—but something much worse. Dinosaurs were simple, mindless animals compared to the city's builders, who were ancient and intelligent. They had existed for nearly a billion years, even before life on Earth had fully formed. These beings didn't just exist alongside early life—they created and controlled it. Without a doubt, they were the very beings hinted at in ancient, terrifying legends like those in the Pnakotic Manuscripts and the Necronomicon. They were the "Old Ones," beings from the stars, shaped by an evolution completely different from anything on Earth. And to think—just the day before, Danforth and I had seen fossilized remains of these creatures with our own eyes. Poor Lake and his team had even seen their full forms.

I can't explain step by step how we pieced together what we learned about their ancient civilization. After the initial shock of realizing the truth, we had to stop for a while to recover. It wasn't until around three in the afternoon that we were able to begin our exploration in a more structured way.

The sculptures in the first building we entered were relatively recent—about two million years old, according to geological, biological, and astronomical clues. The artistic style seemed less advanced than what we later found in much older buildings, which we reached after crossing bridges beneath the ice. One particular structure, carved from solid rock, seemed to date back forty or even fifty million years—perhaps from the late Cretaceous or early Eocene period. Its carvings were stunning, far more detailed than anything else we had seen, except for one even older structure. That, we later agreed, was the oldest inhabited building we explored.

If not for the proof provided by the flashlight images we would soon share, I would hesitate to reveal what we saw and concluded—fearing that people would think I had lost my mind. The earliest parts of this story describe the Old Ones' life on distant planets, in other galaxies, and even in other universes. It would be easy to dismiss those sections as myths created by the creatures themselves. However, some of the designs and diagrams were eerily similar to modern discoveries in mathematics and astrophysics. I don't know what to make of it. Perhaps the photographs I plan to release will let others decide for themselves.

None of the carvings we found told a complete story. The different rooms contained only fragments, and we never came across the events in the correct order. Some rooms seemed to stand alone, telling isolated stories, while others carried a continuous narrative through a series of rooms and hallways.

The most detailed maps and diagrams were found deep underground, far below the city's original floor level. They covered the walls of a massive chamber—about two hundred feet wide and sixty feet high—which seemed to have been an educational center. Many of the same images and records were repeated throughout different rooms and buildings, probably because certain events and historical periods were particularly important to different artists or residents. Sometimes, however, we found different versions of the same story, which helped us clarify confusing details and fill in missing pieces.

It still amazes me that we figured out so much in such a short amount of time. Even now, we only have the roughest outline of what happened—and much of that came later, after carefully analyzing our photos and sketches.

Perhaps it was this later study, combined with our memories and subconscious fears, that led to Danforth's current mental breakdown. There's also that final, terrible thing he claims to have seen— something he still refuses to describe, even to me. But we had no choice. We couldn't properly warn the world without gathering as much information as possible. And warning others is absolutely necessary.

Some unnatural force still lingers in that frozen, alien world. The laws of time and nature don't seem to work the same way there. Whatever remains hidden beneath the ice must never be disturbed again. Further exploration must be stopped.

Chapter VII

The full story, as far as we've been able to understand it, will eventually be published in an official report from Miskatonic University. Here, I'll just give a rough summary of the most important details. Whether myth or truth, the carvings told of how the star-headed beings arrived on Earth when it was still young and lifeless. They came from space, just like other alien explorers that sometimes set out to colonize new worlds.

According to the sculptures, these beings could travel between the stars using their huge, wing-like membranes. This strangely matched an old folk legend I once heard from a historian friend. They spent a lot of time living underwater, where they built strange cities and fought intense battles against unknown enemies. Their weapons and machines worked on principles beyond anything humans understand today. However, they only used their technology when absolutely necessary. Some carvings suggested that they had gone through a highly mechanical phase on other planets but eventually abandoned it because it didn't satisfy them emotionally. Their incredibly strong bodies and simple needs allowed them to live comfortably without relying on advanced machines or even clothing, except when protection was needed.

They first created life on Earth in the oceans, starting with simple organisms they could use for food. Later, they carried out more advanced experiments, especially after defeating various cosmic enemies. This wasn't the first time they had done such things—they had already created life on other planets. Not only did they grow food, but they also engineered strange, shape-shifting creatures that could change their bodies to form temporary organs under hypnotic control. These creatures were perfect workers, capable of performing hard labor for their masters.

There was no doubt that these beings were what Abdul Alhazred described as "Shoggoths" in his terrifying Necronomicon. However, even he never hinted that they had once existed on Earth—he only mentioned them as something seen in drug-induced visions.

Once the Old Ones had created enough food and Shoggoths to serve them, they allowed other types of plant and animal life to evolve for different purposes. They destroyed any creatures that became a problem. With the help of the Shoggoths—who could stretch and change shape to lift massive weights—their small underwater cities grew into huge, complex labyrinths of stone. These looked a lot like the ones they later built on land. The Old Ones had lived on land before, in other parts of the universe, so they probably brought those building traditions with them.

As we studied the architecture of these ancient cities—including the one we were currently walking through—we noticed something strange that we haven't been able to explain. The buildings around us were crumbling ruins, their tops worn away by time. But the carvings on the walls showed what they had originally looked like. They had tall, needle-like spires, delicate decorations on pyramids and cones, and layers of thin, scalloped disks stacked on cylindrical towers.

This was exactly what we had seen earlier in that eerie mirage—the vision of a city that no longer existed, projected across the mountains as we approached Lake's doomed camp. Somehow, the skyline of this dead city had appeared to us, unchanged, even though those structures had been gone for tens of thousands of years.

The history of the Old Ones, both in the ocean and on land, could fill volumes. Those who lived in shallow waters still used the eyes at the tips of their five head tentacles. They developed writing and sculpture like humans did, carving their words with a stylus on waterproof wax.

Deeper in the ocean, where it was too dark to rely on sight, they used glowing creatures to provide light. However, they also had special sensory abilities through tiny, prism-like structures on their heads. These extra senses made them less dependent on light when needed. Over time, their art and writing techniques changed to fit their deep-sea environment. Some sculptures suggested they used chemical coatings, possibly to create glowing symbols, but we couldn't fully understand how it worked.

In the water, they swam using their flexible, arm-like limbs and sometimes propelled themselves by wriggling their lower tentacles. Occasionally, they used their fan-like wings to glide through the sea in long, sweeping motions. On land, they walked using their lower tentacles but could also fly great distances when necessary. Their thin, branching arms were incredibly strong and precise, allowing them to create detailed sculptures and perform delicate tasks with great skill.

Their resilience was almost impossible to believe. Even the extreme pressure at the bottom of the deepest ocean trenches didn't harm them. They seemed to die only from violence, not from old age or natural causes. Their burial sites were rare, but the way they buried their dead disturbed both Danforth and me.

They placed their fallen inside vertical graves and covered them with mounds inscribed with five-pointed symbols. The realization of this made us stop and take a break to recover from the unsettling thoughts it brought to mind.

***

Their strength was almost unbelievable. Even extreme pressure couldn't hurt them!

***

The beings reproduced by releasing spores, much like certain plants, just as Lake had suspected. However, because they were so strong and lived so long, they didn't need to create many new ones—only when they expanded into new areas. Their young grew quickly and received an education far beyond anything we can imagine. Their culture was highly advanced, filled with deep traditions and customs that lasted for ages. While there were some differences between those who lived on land and those in the sea, their way of life remained largely the same.

Even though they could absorb nutrients from minerals like plants do, they preferred organic food, especially meat. Underwater, they ate raw marine creatures, but on land, they cooked their food. They hunted and even raised animals for meat, using sharp weapons to kill them. Our team had already noticed strange markings on fossilized bones, which now made sense.

They could survive in extreme temperatures, even in freezing water. However, when the Ice Age began nearly a million years ago, those living on land had to find ways to stay warm. They used artificial heating for a while, but in the end, the intense cold forced them to retreat back into the ocean.

Long ago, when they traveled through space, legends say they absorbed certain chemicals that made them almost independent of food, air, and temperature. But by the time the Ice Age arrived, they had forgotten how to do this. Even if they had remembered, they couldn't have lived that way forever without consequences.

Since they didn't reproduce in pairs and had a partly plant-like biology, they didn't have families the way mammals do. Instead, they seemed to live in large groups based on comfort, space, and shared interests. The carvings showed scenes of daily life that suggested they formed communities based on intellectual and social bonds rather than biological ties.

Their homes were designed with wide open spaces in the center of large rooms, leaving the walls free for decoration. The land-dwellers used an unknown form of lighting, likely based on electrochemical reactions. Both on land and underwater, they used unique furniture—

tables, chairs, and couches built from cylindrical frames. Instead of lying down, they rested and slept in an upright position, folding their tentacles around themselves. Their books were made of stacked, hinged panels covered in a system of symbols, which they stored on racks.

Their government was complicated and seemed to be somewhat socialist in nature, though we couldn't determine exact details from the carvings. Trade was widespread, both within cities and between different settlements. Small, five-pointed stone tokens, covered in inscriptions, appeared to have been used as currency. It's possible that the smaller green soapstone objects found by our team were pieces of this ancient money.

Although their society was centered around cities, they also practiced farming and raised animals for food. They engaged in mining and some forms of manufacturing. Travel was common, but large-scale migrations were rare, except when they moved to colonize new regions.

For personal movement, they didn't rely on vehicles—they were naturally fast and efficient in the water, air, and on land. However, they did use beasts of burden to carry heavy loads. Underwater, the Shoggoths served this purpose, while on land, they domesticated an unknown type of primitive vertebrate in their later years.

Many of the creatures that evolved on Earth—including animals, plants, and even flying species—came from life forms they had originally created. Over time, these organisms evolved on their own, beyond the Old Ones' direct control. As long as they didn't interfere with the dominant race, they were left alone. Any species that became a threat was wiped out.

One of the most surprising discoveries in the carvings was a depiction of an early mammal—a clumsy, primitive creature that the

Old Ones sometimes ate and sometimes kept around for amusement. Its vaguely human-like features were unmistakable.

When building their cities, they used massive stone blocks for their towering structures. These blocks were lifted into place by enormous pterodactyl-like creatures, a species completely unknown to modern science.

The fact that the Old Ones survived countless geological changes and natural disasters was almost miraculous. Though none of their earliest cities seemed to have lasted beyond the oldest known rock layers, their civilization never collapsed. Their knowledge and records were carefully preserved and passed down through the ages.

Their first arrival on Earth was in the Antarctic Ocean, shortly after the event that created the moon. One of the maps we found showed the entire planet covered in water at that time, with stone cities spreading further from Antarctica over millions of years.

Another map revealed an enormous landmass around the South Pole. Some of the Old Ones had attempted settlements there, but their main cities remained in the deep sea. Later maps showed the land breaking apart, with sections drifting northward. These carvings closely matched the modern theories of continental drift proposed by Taylor, Wegener, and Joly, confirming that the Old Ones had witnessed—and recorded—the slow movement of Earth's landmasses over time.

When new land rose in the South Pacific, major events unfolded. Some of the Old Ones' underwater cities were destroyed beyond repair, but that wasn't the worst of it. A new species—strange, octopus-like beings that might have been the legendary spawn of Cthulhu—arrived from the depths of space. They waged a brutal war against the Old Ones, forcing them to retreat completely into the ocean. This was a huge loss, as they had been steadily expanding their settlements on land.

Eventually, a peace agreement was reached. The Cthulhu beings took control of the new land, while the Old Ones kept their underwater cities and the older continents. The Old Ones also built new land cities, the greatest of which was in Antarctica, since that was where they had first arrived. Over time, Antarctica remained the heart of their civilization, and all the cities the Cthulhu creatures had built there were wiped out.

Then, suddenly, the lands in the Pacific sank beneath the ocean, taking the terrifying stone city of R'lyeh and all the Cthulhu beings with it. Once again, the Old Ones became the dominant species on the planet—though there was one lingering fear they refused to speak of.

As time went on, their cities spread across both land and sea. This is why I later recommended that archaeologists conduct deep excavations in certain areas using Pabodie's drilling technology.

The Old Ones gradually shifted from living in the ocean to settling on land, a movement encouraged by the rise of new continents. However, they never completely abandoned the sea. One reason for this change was the increasing difficulty of controlling the Shoggoths, which were essential for underwater life.

As time passed, the sculptures revealed a troubling truth: the Old Ones had lost the ability to create new life from non-living materials. Instead, they had to reshape and modify existing creatures. On land, they found that the great reptiles were easy to manage. However, in the ocean, the Shoggoths—able to split apart to reproduce and slowly becoming more intelligent—became a major threat.

Originally, the Shoggoths obeyed the Old Ones through hypnosis, shaping their jelly-like bodies into useful temporary limbs and organs as needed. But over time, they began changing their forms on their own, sometimes imitating past commands. They seemed to have developed a basic form of intelligence, making them unpredictable and difficult to control.

The carvings of the Shoggoths horrified both Danforth and me. These creatures had no fixed shape, appearing as enormous, bubbling masses of slime, usually around fifteen feet across when in a round form. But they could stretch, grow, or shrink at will, forming temporary eyes, ears, and mouths. Sometimes, they did this on their own, and other times they followed the orders of their masters.

They became especially difficult to control around the middle of the Permian period, about 150 million years ago. At that point, the Old Ones fought a massive war to bring them back under control. The sculptures showed terrifying images of the battles, where the Shoggoths left behind piles of slimy, headless corpses. Even though millions of years had passed, the images still filled us with dread.

The Old Ones used advanced molecular-disrupting weapons against the rebellious Shoggoths and eventually won. After that, the carvings showed scenes of Shoggoths being trained and tamed, much like how wild horses were broken in by cowboys. Although some Shoggoths had learned to survive on land during their rebellion, the Old Ones never encouraged this, since managing them outside the water would have been too difficult.

During the Jurassic period, another major crisis occurred. This time, the Old Ones were invaded by beings from space once again—creatures that were part fungus, part crustacean. These aliens seemed to match old legends from northern regions, particularly the stories of the Mi-Go, or Abominable Snowmen, from the Himalayas.

To fight this new enemy, the Old Ones attempted to return to space for the first time since their arrival on Earth. But despite their efforts, they found that they could no longer leave the planet's atmosphere. Whatever technology had once allowed them to travel between the stars was now lost.

In the end, the Mi-Go drove the Old Ones out of the northern lands, though they could not challenge those living in the sea. Over time, the Old Ones retreated further and further south, gradually returning to their original homeland in Antarctica.

As we studied the carvings, we noticed something strange. Both the Cthulhu creatures and the Mi-Go seemed to be made of materials far more alien than even the Old Ones. They had abilities that allowed them to change their forms and reconstruct themselves in ways the Old Ones could not. This suggested that they had come from even more distant parts of the universe, perhaps beyond anything humans could understand.

The Old Ones, despite their unusual biology, were still bound by the physical laws of this universe. This meant they had likely originated from within the known dimensions of space and time. In contrast, the true origins of the other beings were impossible to determine and could only be guessed at with deep unease. Of course, it's possible that the Old Ones had their own biases. They may have shaped history to justify their occasional defeats, as their records showed a strong sense of pride. It was also telling that their carvings made no mention of certain powerful civilizations that appeared in other obscure legends.

The changes in Earth's geography over millions of years were captured with stunning detail in the sculptures. Some of these images challenged existing scientific theories, while others strongly supported them.

For example, the idea proposed by Taylor, Wegener, and Joly—that all continents were once part of a single landmass that broke apart and drifted due to centrifugal force—was strikingly confirmed by the maps we found. Scientists had long noted how the coastlines of Africa and South America seemed to fit together, as well as how major mountain ranges appeared to have been pushed up by this movement. The carvings suggested that the Old Ones had actually witnessed this process over millions of years.

One particular map, seemingly from the Carboniferous period over a hundred million years ago, showed early fractures in the Earth's surface. These cracks would later separate Africa from the once-connected landmasses of Europe, Asia, the Americas, and Antarctica. The evidence was undeniable—these ancient beings had seen the slow but unstoppable drift of the continents firsthand.

Other maps—especially one showing the founding of the massive, now-dead city around us fifty million years ago—clearly displayed the continents as we know them today. The most recent map we found, likely from the Pliocene epoch, showed an Earth that closely resembled the present day. However, it still depicted Alaska connected to Siberia, North America linked to Europe through Greenland, and South America attached to Antarctica via Graham Land.

An earlier map from the Carboniferous period showed that the entire planet, including both land and ocean floors, was covered with the Old Ones' enormous stone cities. But as time passed, later maps revealed their gradual retreat toward Antarctica.

The final Pliocene-era map we found showed that, by that time, their civilization had nearly vanished. No land cities remained outside of Antarctica and the southern tip of South America. In the oceans, none of their settlements existed beyond the 50th parallel south. It was clear that their knowledge of and interest in the northern regions had completely faded. They may have still studied coastlines during long-distance exploration flights using their wing-like membranes, but beyond that, they had abandoned the rest of the world.

Many records detailed the destruction of their cities due to earthquakes, the rise of mountains, the shifting of continents, and other natural disasters. What was most striking, however, was how they built fewer and fewer new cities as time went on.

The enormous, lifeless city surrounding us seemed to be their last great stronghold. It had been constructed early in the Cretaceous period, following a massive geological upheaval that destroyed an even larger city not far from this location.

This area appeared to be the most sacred place of all—the spot where the very first Old Ones had originally settled when they arrived on the ocean floor. According to the carvings, the newer city contained certain sacred stones that had once been part of that first underwater settlement. Over millions of years, these stones had been buried deep underground, only to resurface as the Earth's crust shifted and folded over time.

Chapter VIII

Danforth and I were especially fascinated by everything related to the area we were exploring. There was an overwhelming amount of information about this region, and we examined it with a mix of awe and dread.

At ground level, among the ruined and tangled streets, we were fortunate to find a relatively recent building. Though partially damaged by a nearby fault, its walls contained carvings that, while less skillfully made, told the story of this place far beyond what we had learned from the Pliocene map. This was the last site we studied in detail—what we found there led us to a new, urgent objective.

We were certain that this was one of the most bizarre, eerie, and terrifying places on Earth. It was older than any other known land, and as we spent more time there, we became convinced that this desolate plateau was the same nightmare landscape described in ancient legends. Even the author of the Necronomicon, who had written about countless horrors, had avoided discussing it in detail.

The massive mountain range stretched across nearly the entire continent, starting as a low ridge near Luitpold Land on the Weddell Sea and continuing in an enormous arc. The highest peaks ran from approximately 82° South, 60° East to 70° South, 115° East. Their concave side faced our camp, while their seaward end reached the ice-locked coast that explorers like Wilkes and Mawson had glimpsed from the Antarctic Circle.

But even more monstrous landscapes seemed to lurk beyond. I had already mentioned that these peaks were taller than the Himalayas, but the carvings suggested that they were not the tallest mountains on Earth. That dreadful title belonged to something so terrifying that many of the sculptures avoided depicting it altogether, while others portrayed it with clear fear and reluctance.

According to the records, there was one part of the ancient world—one of the very first lands to rise from the ocean after the Earth formed the Moon and the Old Ones arrived from the stars—that had come to be feared and avoided. Cities built there crumbled far earlier than they should have, mysteriously abandoned without explanation.

Then, during the great upheavals of the Comanchean Age, a catastrophic shift in the Earth's crust caused a terrifying new mountain range to erupt from the ground with unimaginable force and noise. These mountains, the tallest and most dreadful the planet had ever seen, were born in an instant of chaos.

If the carvings were accurate, these cursed peaks stood over 40,000 feet high—far taller than even the towering mountains we had already crossed. They stretched from roughly 77° South, 70° East to 70° South, 100° East, less than 300 miles from the dead city. If not for the strange, hazy mist in the west, we might have seen their terrifying peaks in the distance. Their northernmost points should also have been visible from the coastline of Queen Mary Land, near the Antarctic Circle.

In the later years of their civilization, some of the Old Ones had prayed to these mountains in strange and desperate ways. Yet none ever dared to go near them, and they never recorded what lay beyond. No human had ever set eyes on them, and as I studied the emotions carved into the walls, I silently hoped that no one ever would.

Fortunately, the coast beyond these mountains was shielded by other highlands—Queen Mary and Kaiser Wilhelm Lands—and I was grateful that no one had yet attempted to climb them. I was no longer as skeptical as I once had been about old legends and superstitions. I could no longer laugh at the idea that lightning seemed to pause meaningfully over the mountain peaks, or that an eerie, unexplained glow was said to shine from one of them throughout the long Antarctic night. Perhaps there was some truth in the ancient whispers about Kadath in the Cold Waste.

Even the land immediately around us was strange, though not as cursed as the distant peaks. Not long after the city was founded, the mountain range became the site of the Old Ones' most important temples. Many of the carvings showed towering, grotesque structures that once pierced the sky, where now only the weathered remains of stone cubes and walls clung to the mountainsides.

Over the ages, caves had formed in the mountains and were gradually shaped into temple extensions. Later, as even more time passed, underground water carved out the limestone, turning the entire region into a vast, interconnected system of tunnels and caverns. The carvings told stories of deep explorations into these tunnels and of the final, chilling discovery—the existence of a pitch-black, sunless sea hidden in the depths of the Earth.

**

This enormous, dark abyss had most likely been carved out over time by a massive river that once flowed from the terrifying, unnamed mountains in the west. Originally, this river had changed course near the Old Ones' mountain range, then continued alongside it before emptying into the Indian Ocean near Budd and Totten Lands on Wilkes' coastline. Over time, as it eroded the limestone base of the foothills, its waters eventually merged with underground caverns, creating an even deeper chasm.

At some point, the river completely drained into the hollow hills, leaving its original path dry. Much of the city we explored had been built on top of what was once the riverbed. The Old Ones, understanding what had happened, used their artistic skills to carve intricate stone pillars into the hillsides where the great river had once plunged into eternal darkness.

The river had once been crossed by many grand stone bridges, and its dry course had been visible from our aerial survey. The river's placement in different carvings throughout the city helped us piece together a timeline of its history. Using these details, we were able to sketch a rough but careful map, marking key locations such as city squares, important buildings, and other landmarks that would guide our future explorations.

With this information, we could imagine how the city had looked millions of years ago. The sculptures gave us a vivid picture of its buildings, streets, towering mountains, bustling squares, and surrounding landscapes filled with lush prehistoric vegetation. It must have been a breathtakingly beautiful and mysterious place. For a moment, I almost forgot the overwhelming sense of unease that its massive, ancient, and lifeless ruins cast over me.

Yet the carvings also revealed that the Old Ones themselves had once known fear. A recurring scene showed them recoiling in terror from something—something never actually depicted in the sculptures. This unknown object had been carried down the river from the distant, vine-covered cycad forests of those dreadful western mountains. Whatever it was, it must have been horrifying enough to shake even these powerful beings.

Only in a late-built house with cruder carvings did we find the first hints of the disaster that led to the city's abandonment. There were undoubtedly more sculptures of this era elsewhere, though time and hardship had likely reduced the Old Ones' ability to create art. In fact, we soon found clear evidence that similar records existed in other places. But this was the first—and, at that moment, the only—set we had discovered.

We had planned to search further, but something we found forced us to shift our priorities. Regardless, there would have been limits to what we could find. After all, once the Old Ones lost hope that they could remain in the city, they would have stopped creating new murals altogether. The final disaster, of course, was the arrival of the great cold—the ice age that covered much of the world and has never left the cursed polar regions. This was the same deadly freeze that wiped out the legendary lands of Lomar and Hyperborea at the other end of the Earth.

It is difficult to say exactly when this deep freeze began in Antarctica. Scientists today estimate that the great ice ages started about 500,000 years ago, but at the poles, the freezing must have started much earlier. While any attempt to put an exact date on the Old Ones' final years is guesswork, it's likely that the city was abandoned long before the official start of the Pleistocene. The cruder carvings we found were probably made less than a million years ago, when the Old Ones were already struggling to survive.

These late carvings showed clear signs of thinning vegetation and a decline in country life. Homes were depicted with heating systems, and travelers were shown wrapped in protective clothing to survive the growing cold. A series of carved panels—unusually fragmented for this era—revealed a steady migration toward warmer places. Some Old Ones fled to undersea cities far off the coast, while others moved into deep networks of limestone caves that led down to the black abyss of underground waters.

In the end, it seemed that the abyss became the main refuge. This may have been partly because of its long-held sacred status, but there was likely a more practical reason as well. The caves allowed them to continue using their grand mountain temples, and the city above remained useful as a summer home and a base for accessing important mines.

To make the transition easier, they improved the routes connecting their old city to their new underwater home. They even carved direct tunnels from the city into the abyss—steep, downward shafts whose entrances we carefully marked on our map. We estimated that at least two of these tunnels were close enough for us to reach—one less than a quarter mile from the ancient riverbed, and the other about twice that distance in the opposite direction.

The abyss itself had some dry shores in certain areas, but the Old Ones built their new city beneath the water, likely because the deep sea maintained a steady warmth. The depth of the hidden ocean must have been immense, allowing heat from the Earth's core to keep it habitable for an endless period of time.

It seemed that the Old Ones had little difficulty adapting to life underwater full-time. They had never allowed their gills to stop functioning, so returning to the ocean was not a struggle. The carvings showed that they had frequently visited their underwater relatives in other parts of the world and had regularly bathed at the bottom of their great river.

Even the total darkness of the underground sea would not have been a problem for them. After all, they had already adapted to the long, endless nights of the Antarctic.

Even though the carvings were less refined than earlier works, they still had a grand and dramatic quality when they told the story of the new city built in the underground sea. The Old Ones approached the project with scientific precision, carefully extracting strong, insoluble rock from the mountains and bringing in skilled workers from their nearest underwater city to construct it using the best methods available.

These workers arrived fully prepared, bringing everything they needed to establish the new settlement. They carried Shoggoth tissue to grow powerful creatures that could lift massive stone blocks and serve as laborers in the cavern city. They also brought other forms of living material, which they shaped into glowing organisms to provide light in the darkness.

In time, a magnificent metropolis rose from the depths of that black, sunless sea. Its architecture closely resembled that of the city above, and because of the strict mathematical precision required in construction, its craftsmanship remained relatively strong despite the decline in artistic quality.

The newly created Shoggoths grew to enormous sizes and displayed an unusual level of intelligence. They were shown in the carvings as following commands with remarkable speed and efficiency. Unlike in earlier times, when they were controlled mainly by hypnotic suggestion, these Shoggoths seemed to communicate with the Old Ones through sound—repeating their masters' voices in a strange, musical piping. This appeared to match the findings from Lake's dissection, suggesting that the creatures relied more on spoken orders than on mental control.

Despite their intelligence, the Shoggoths remained obedient. The glowing organisms illuminated the city well, making up for the loss of the polar auroras that had once lit the skies above their land city.

Even though art and decoration continued, there was a noticeable decline in quality. The Old Ones seemed aware of this themselves. In many cases, they tried to preserve their past artistic achievements by relocating some of the finest stone carvings from their land city—just as Emperor Constantine had once taken the best sculptures from Greece and Asia to decorate his new capital in Byzantium. However, they did not move as many sculptures as they could have, likely because they had not completely abandoned the land city at first.

By the time they did leave it behind entirely—long before the Antarctic Ice Age was fully developed—they may have grown used to their declining art, or perhaps they no longer recognized the superior quality of the older carvings. Whatever the reason, the ruins surrounding us had not been completely stripped of their artwork, though all the best statues and portable objects had been taken away.

The last carvings we found, created in the final days of the city, painted a clear picture of the Old Ones' way of life in those years. They spent summers in the land city and winters in the underground sea city. Occasionally, they traded with other cities at the bottom of the ocean, far off the Antarctic coast.

By this time, they must have known that their land city was doomed. The carvings showed clear signs of worsening conditions. The cold was becoming relentless, and snow no longer melted completely in the summer months. Vegetation was dying, and most of the reptilian livestock had perished. Even the mammals were struggling to survive.

To keep things running on land, the Old Ones were forced to adapt some of their Shoggoths to survive in the cold—a step they had previously resisted. The once-thriving river had dried up, and the surface ocean had become lifeless, except for seals and whales. All the birds had left, except for the strange, oversized penguins.

What happened after that, we could only guess. How long had the sea-cavern city lasted? Was it still down there, an empty shell in eternal darkness? Had the underground sea eventually frozen? What became of the Old Ones' other ocean cities? Had any of them escaped to the north, ahead of the advancing ice?

There is no evidence in modern geology that they survived. Had the terrifying Mi-Go remained a threat in the northern lands? And even now, could something still lurk in the lightless depths of the Earth's deepest oceans?

The Old Ones were incredibly resilient, seemingly unaffected by extreme pressure. Over the years, sailors have occasionally brought up strange objects from the sea. And has the "killer whale" theory truly explained the mysterious wounds found on Antarctic seals, first noticed by explorer Borchgrevink a generation ago?

The ancient specimens that poor Lake found had nothing to do with these speculations, as they were far older. Based on where they were discovered, they must have lived at least 30 million years ago, during an earlier period in the city's history. At that time, the underground sea and the cavern city had not yet formed.

These creatures had once lived in a very different world—one filled with lush forests and thriving plant life. They had walked through a younger, flourishing city, surrounded by great works of art, with a mighty river flowing north toward a distant, tropical ocean.

And yet, we could not stop thinking about those specimens— especially the eight perfectly preserved ones that had vanished from Lake's ravaged campsite. The entire situation felt unnatural. The strange things we had tried so hard to explain as madness. The horrifyingly disturbed graves. The missing materials. The disappearance of Gedney. The incredible toughness of these ancient beings. And now, the unsettling revelations in the sculptures—hints of bizarre, unexplained traits within their species.

Danforth and I had seen too much in just a few hours. We were now prepared to believe, and remain silent about, many terrifying and unbelievable secrets of the ancient world.

Chapter IX

Our study of the late carvings led us to change our plans. We had discovered something we hadn't known before—the tunnels leading deep into a hidden underground world. Now that we were aware of them, we couldn't resist the urge to explore.

Based on the size of the carvings, we estimated that walking about a mile down either of the nearby tunnels would bring us to the edge of massive, pitch-black cliffs overlooking the abyss. Below these cliffs, paths carved by the Old Ones led down to the rocky shores of a vast, hidden ocean. The idea of seeing this mysterious place with our own eyes was too tempting to ignore. But we had to act fast if we wanted to reach it before our supplies ran out.

It was already 8 p.m., and we didn't have an unlimited supply of batteries for our flashlights. We had used them for nearly five hours while studying and taking notes beneath the ice, and even with their long-lasting dry cell formula, they had only about four more hours of power left. To conserve energy, we decided to keep one flashlight off and use it only in particularly dark or detailed areas.

We couldn't risk running out of light in these vast underground tunnels. So, to reach the abyss, we had to stop all further attempts at deciphering the murals. Of course, we planned to return later—perhaps for weeks—bringing better equipment for photography and study. But at that moment, we had to move quickly.

Our supply of paper for marking our trail was limited, and we didn't want to waste our sketchbooks. However, we sacrificed one large notebook to ensure we could find our way back. If we became completely lost, we could try chipping markings into the stone. And if all else failed, we could always make our way up to the surface through trial and error, as long as we had enough time.

With that settled, we eagerly set off toward the closest tunnel.

According to the carvings we had studied, the entrance to the tunnel should be less than a quarter mile away. The path leading to it seemed clear, lined with solid-looking buildings that might still be accessible below the ice. The tunnel itself was located in the basement of a massive, five-pointed structure, which appeared to have had an important public or ceremonial purpose. We tried to recall seeing it during our aerial survey of the ruins, but nothing came to mind.

This likely meant that the upper parts of the structure had collapsed or been completely destroyed by a deep crack in the ice we had noticed earlier. If that were the case, the tunnel might be blocked, and we would have to try the next closest one—about a mile to the north.

The old riverbed cut us off from any tunnels to the south, so if both of our chosen paths were blocked, we would have no choice but to turn back. We weren't sure if our flashlight batteries would last long enough to make an attempt at the next tunnel beyond that, which was another mile away.

Using our map and compass, we carefully navigated through the ruins. We moved through rooms and hallways, some still intact and others in complete ruin. We climbed ramps, crossed upper floors and bridges, then descended again. Some doorways were blocked by debris, while others led us through eerily well-preserved corridors. We occasionally took wrong turns, retraced our steps, and removed misplaced trail markers when needed. Every so often, we came across a broken shaft where daylight trickled in from above.

As we neared the spot where we expected to find the tunnel entrance, we crossed a second-story bridge that led us to the pointed edge of a ruined wall. From there, we descended into a long corridor. The walls here were covered in elaborate but strangely crude carvings, likely from the city's final years. Many of these images seemed to have religious significance.

Then, at around 8:30 p.m., Danforth suddenly tensed. His sharp sense of smell had picked up something strange.

If we had brought a dog with us, we probably would have been warned earlier. At first, we couldn't quite identify what was wrong. The air, which had been crisp and pure, now carried a faint but unmistakable scent. After a few moments, we both recognized it—though we wished we hadn't.

There was a smell, and it was disturbingly familiar. It reminded us of the awful stench that had nearly made us sick when we opened the nightmarish grave of the thing Lake had dissected.

At the time, we didn't fully grasp what this meant. There were several possible explanations, and we whispered back and forth, unsure of what to do. Most importantly, we didn't turn back. We had come too far to let anything stop us without undeniable proof of danger.

And besides, what we suspected was too wild to be true. Things like that simply didn't happen in the real world.

Still, something deep inside told us to be cautious. We dimmed our only flashlight, no longer tempted by the strange, almost menacing carvings that loomed on the walls. We slowed our pace, moving as quietly as possible, stepping lightly over the scattered rubble.

Danforth's eyes were sharper than mine, and he was also the first to notice something strange about the debris on the floor. As we passed several archways leading to rooms and corridors, we realized that something wasn't right.

The ruins looked disturbed. The scattered debris did not look as it should after thousands of years of abandonment. When we turned up our flashlight slightly to examine it, we saw what seemed to be a path cut through the dust and rubble—as if something had moved through recently.

The irregular nature of the marks made it impossible to determine exactly what had passed through. But in the smoother areas, we saw faint signs of something heavy being dragged. At one point, there was even a suggestion of parallel tracks, almost like sled runners.

This discovery made us stop in our tracks.

As we stood there, frozen in place, we both noticed something else at the same time—another smell, coming from up ahead.

This time, it was both less and more terrifying. On its own, it was ordinary. But in this setting, given what we knew, it was absolutely horrifying.

It was the unmistakable scent of gasoline.

***

What drove us forward after that moment is something for psychologists to explain. We knew that whatever horror had occurred at the camp had somehow made its way into this ancient, buried city. There was no longer any doubt—something terrifying had been here recently, or might still be just ahead. Yet despite the fear, we couldn't stop ourselves. Whether it was curiosity, a sense of duty toward Gedney, or some hypnotic pull, we continued.

Danforth whispered about the strange footprint he thought he had seen back at the ruins above. He also mentioned the faint, musical piping sound he thought he had heard from the depths below. The noise was unsettling, especially in light of what Lake had discovered in his dissection. Even though it could have been nothing more than an echo from the wind rushing through the caves, the possibility that it was something more made our situation even worse.

I, in turn, whispered my own thoughts—the way we had found the camp, the missing items, and the possibility that a single, crazed survivor had attempted something unthinkable. Had someone really crossed those monstrous mountains and descended into this lost city? The idea was impossible, yet we couldn't dismiss it completely.

Still, neither of us could convince the other—or even ourselves—of anything definite. We stood there in the dark, our flashlights turned off, and noticed that a faint trace of light filtered down from above. It wasn't much, but it kept the blackness from being absolute.

Almost without thinking, we started moving again, guiding ourselves with brief flashes of the flashlight. The disturbed debris around us made us uneasy, and the gasoline smell grew even stronger. The further we went, the more destruction we saw. Soon, it became clear that our path was about to be blocked. Our earlier suspicion had been correct—the ice rift we had seen from the air had indeed collapsed this tunnel. We wouldn't be able to reach the basement where the entrance to the abyss lay.

As our flashlight beam swept over the grotesquely carved walls of the ruined corridor, we noticed several doorways, some more obstructed than others. From one of these openings, the smell of gasoline was overpowering, completely masking the other strange odor we had noticed earlier.

Looking closer, we saw something chilling—this particular doorway had been recently cleared of debris. Someone or something had moved through here not long ago. Whatever was lurking in the ruins, we now knew exactly where it had gone.

It would be understandable if we had turned back then. Instead, we stood motionless, hesitating before taking another step forward.

When we finally entered the darkened archway, our first reaction was unexpected—it was almost disappointing. Inside was a wide chamber, a near-perfect cube about twenty feet across, its walls covered in the same ancient carvings. But at first glance, there was nothing recent inside. There were no obvious signs of movement, and no other exit leading further in.

Then Danforth's sharp eyes spotted something on the floor—disturbed debris.

We turned both flashlights to full power, scanning the area. What we found was small and seemingly unimportant, yet it sent a chill through us.

The floor had been roughly cleared, and scattered across it were small objects. In one corner, a large amount of gasoline had been spilled recently enough for its strong smell to linger, even at this high-altitude, ice-covered plateau. There was no doubt about it—this had been a temporary camp, set up by others who, like us, had reached this point only to find their way blocked.

There was no mistaking the source of these objects. Everything had come from Lake's camp.

The items included tin cans, opened in the same strange way as those we had seen back at the ruined encampment. There were many burnt-out matches, three illustrated books, their pages smudged and dirty, an empty ink bottle, its original packaging still beside it, a broken fountain pen, torn pieces of fur and tent fabric, a used flashlight battery, a folded instruction sheet from a tent heater, and a scattering of crumpled papers.

It was unsettling enough to see these familiar things in such a place. But when we smoothed out the papers and looked at them, we realized we had reached the worst moment yet.

At Lake's camp, we had found strange, unreadable papers—covered in blotted markings. Those should have prepared us for this, yet nothing could have lessened the impact of seeing them here, deep in this nightmarish city.

Some of the papers contained groups of dots, similar to the markings found on the greenish soapstone tablets. A mad Gedney might have drawn them, just as someone might have crudely copied the strange symbols carved on the five-pointed graves at the camp.

There were also rough, hurried sketches—some more accurate than others—showing different sections of the ruined city. One of them traced a path from an unknown circular location to the five-pointed structure we now stood in. We identified this location as a great cylindrical tower depicted in the carvings, which we had also glimpsed from the air as a massive circular pit.

It was possible—just barely—that Gedney had made these drawings. They were clearly based on carvings from elsewhere in the ruins, different from the ones we had studied. But there was one thing that was completely impossible.

The style.

These sketches, though done quickly and carelessly, were not drawn by an untrained hand. Their technique was too precise, too confident—better, in some ways, than the declining artwork of the city's final years. The drawings carried the unmistakable touch of the Old Ones themselves, the same style used when the city was at its peak.

Many would say that we should have fled right then. After all, our suspicions—no matter how unbelievable—were now fully confirmed. Anyone who had read our story this far would already understand what we had realized in that moment.

Maybe we were mad for staying. After all, I have already called these towering peaks the "mountains of madness." But perhaps the same impulse that drives explorers to track deadly animals in the jungle also pushed us forward. Terror had nearly paralyzed us, yet something deeper—some burning mix of awe and curiosity—won in the end.

Of course, we had no intention of confronting whatever had been here. We were certain it had already moved on.

By now, it must have reached the other entrance to the abyss and passed inside, disappearing into the endless darkness. If that entrance was also blocked, then it must have continued north, searching for another way down.

We remembered that these beings—whoever, or whatever, they were—did not rely on light the way we did.

Thinking back, I can hardly recall exactly how our thoughts and feelings shifted in that moment. Our focus had changed, making us feel a heightened sense of anticipation. We had no plans to face whatever danger might be ahead, yet deep down, we may have secretly hoped to catch a glimpse of something—from a place where we could stay hidden and safe.

We had not abandoned our goal of reaching the abyss, but now another objective had emerged. The sketches we found pointed us toward a massive, circular structure. We recognized it immediately as one of the enormous cylindrical towers from the carvings, though from above, it appeared only as a gigantic, round hole.

Something about its design—despite the roughness of the sketches—made us think that the lower levels of this tower must still be significant. It might contain architectural wonders we hadn't seen before. According to the carvings, it was one of the oldest structures in the city, built during its earliest days. If its carvings were still intact, they could reveal incredible information. Additionally, this place might provide a more direct connection to the surface, a shorter route than the one we had been marking with our paper trail. It was likely the same path that others—whoever they were—had taken to descend into the depths.

So we made our decision. We carefully studied the sketches, confirming that they matched our own map, and set out toward the circular tower. The path we followed had already been traveled twice before—by those unknown beings. Beyond that tower, we knew, lay the other entrance to the abyss.

There is little need to describe our journey. It was much like the route we had taken before, except this time, we stayed closer to ground level, even descending into basement corridors at times. We continued to mark our trail with paper, using it sparingly so we wouldn't run out.

Along the way, we occasionally saw disturbing marks in the dust and rubble beneath our feet. After we had moved beyond the lingering scent of gasoline, we once again caught faint traces—sporadically—of that other, more horrible odor.

Whenever we reached a section of the ruins that branched away from our previous route, we would sometimes let the flashlight beam sweep across the walls. Almost every surface was covered in carvings.

It seemed that art had been one of the Old Ones' primary forms of expression.

At about 9:30 p.m., we entered a long, vaulted corridor where the floor was covered in thick ice. The tunnel felt lower than ground level, and as we advanced, the ceiling grew lower as well. Then, ahead of us, we saw something remarkable—strong daylight shining through an opening. We turned off our flashlight, realizing we must be approaching the massive circular space from the sketches. The fact that daylight could reach this spot meant that we weren't far from the surface.

The corridor ended in an archway—surprisingly low for a city built on such a massive scale. Even before stepping through, we could see an enormous round chamber stretching out before us.

The space was at least two hundred feet across, filled with rubble, and surrounded by blocked archways like the one we had just entered. The walls were covered in a bold, spiraling band of sculpted figures— massive and impressive despite the damage caused by exposure to the elements. This artwork was more detailed and striking than anything we had seen before.

The floor was covered in thick ice, and we had the impression that the real bottom of the chamber lay deeper below. But what caught our attention the most was the enormous stone ramp.

It began at the base of the wall, curving outward into the open floor before spiraling upward along the massive cylindrical walls. It reminded us of the ramps that once wound around the towering ziggurats of ancient Babylon. The only reason we had not noticed this structure from the air was that its angle had blended into the walls, making it appear as though the tower had no interior descent. Because of this, we had searched for another route to the lower levels, not realizing that this ramp had been here all along.

If Pabodie had been with us, he might have explained the engineering behind it. Danforth and I could only marvel at how such a massive structure had remained intact. There were large stone supports and pillars placed at intervals, but they hardly seemed enough to keep the ramp standing.

Yet, somehow, it had endured. Even with its exposure to the elements, it remained well-preserved. The walls of the tower had protected it from the worst of the ice and wind, and because of that, the bizarre and unsettling carvings decorating its surface had survived in relatively good condition.

Stepping into this vast, half-lit chamber was awe-inspiring. This structure was at least fifty million years old—without a doubt, the oldest building we had ever seen. The ramp rose up sixty feet along the curved walls, and we remembered from our aerial survey that the outside glacier was about forty feet thick at this location. The gaping hole we had seen from the plane had been at the top of a mound of collapsed ruins, partially enclosed by a ring of higher structures.

According to the carvings, this tower had once stood in the center of a huge circular plaza. In its prime, it had likely been five to six hundred feet tall, with rows of thin spires along its rim and horizontal disk-shaped platforms near its top.

Over time, most of the tower had collapsed outward rather than inward—a lucky event, since if the rubble had fallen inward, the ramp might have been destroyed, and the entire interior could have been completely buried. As it was, the ramp had taken some damage, but the space was still accessible. Many of the archways had been partially cleared, confirming that others had passed through here before.

It didn't take us long to conclude that this was indeed the path they had taken into the depths. If they had descended this way, it made sense for us to use it to return to the surface. Though we had left a long paper trail elsewhere, this tower was no farther from the foothills and our waiting plane than the terraced building we had originally entered. If we planned to explore more of the underground ruins on this trip, this would be the best place to continue.

Strangely, despite all we had seen and suspected, we were still thinking about future expeditions.

Then, as we carefully picked our way across the rubble-strewn floor, we saw something that pushed all other thoughts aside.

In the farthest corner of the ramp's lower section, hidden from view until now, we spotted a neat row of three sledges.

They were the missing sledges from Lake's camp.

They had been roughly handled, showing signs of being dragged across long distances of stone ruins and debris. In some places, they must have been carried by hand over terrain where they couldn't be pulled.

Despite this, they were carefully packed and strapped down. We immediately recognized their contents: a gasoline stove, fuel cans, instrument cases, food tins, tarpaulins—some stuffed with books, others with unknown supplies. Everything had come from Lake's expedition.

After what we had already found in the ruined chamber, we were somewhat prepared for this discovery.

But the real shock came when we stepped forward and unfastened one of the tarpaulins.

Something about its shape had unsettled us, and when we peeled it back, our worst fears were confirmed.

Whoever had taken these sledges had also collected samples.

Inside, frozen stiff, completely intact, and carefully wrapped to avoid damage, were the bodies of young Gedney and the missing dog.

Chapter X

Some may think we were both heartless and insane for turning our thoughts toward the northern tunnel and the abyss so soon after discovering Gedney's body. Perhaps we wouldn't have done so if not for something unexpected that suddenly interrupted us and led our minds in a new direction.

After covering Gedney again with the tarp, we stood in silence, overwhelmed and uncertain. That was when the sound finally reached us—the first real noise we had heard since leaving the surface, where the wind howled faintly over the towering mountains. The sound itself was nothing strange or unnatural, yet hearing it in this lifeless place was more shocking and disturbing than any eerie, otherworldly noise could have been. It shattered everything we had come to believe about this ancient, empty world.

Had it been the strange, musical piping that Lake had mentioned in his report—the sound we had almost imagined in every gust of wind since finding the ruined camp—it would have at least made some twisted kind of sense. Such a noise would have belonged in a graveyard of lost ages.

But this was something else entirely, something so familiar that it felt completely out of place. It was not some ancient horror stirring in the depths of the abyss. Instead, it was a sound we had heard countless times before during our journey along the Antarctic coast.

It was the loud, squawking call of a penguin.

The muffled sound echoed from beneath the ice, coming from a direction nearly opposite the corridor we had entered. It was near the path leading toward the northern tunnel—the second entrance to the abyss.

The presence of a living seabird in such a place, where the surface had been lifeless for countless ages, could mean only one thing. We needed to confirm what we were hearing. The sound came again, and this time, it seemed to be coming from more than one bird.

Following the noise, we entered an archway where much of the debris had been cleared away. Before stepping fully into the darkness, we took extra paper from one of the sledges to use for marking our trail. There was something unsettling about taking supplies from the same bundles that had covered Gedney, but we had no other choice.

As the icy floor gave way to scattered rubble, we noticed odd, dragging tracks on the ground. Then, Danforth spotted something that made him freeze. He had found a clear footprint—one we knew all too well.

The penguin cries led us exactly where our map and compass had already directed us—toward the northern tunnel entrance. We were relieved to find a clear path at ground level, meaning we wouldn't need to search for an intact bridge or climb through unstable ruins.

According to our map, the tunnel should begin beneath a massive, pyramid-shaped building. We vaguely remembered seeing such a structure from the air—it had been one of the best-preserved ruins in the city. Along the way, our flashlight revealed more of the endless carvings covering the walls, but we didn't stop to examine them.

Then, a large white shape suddenly appeared ahead of us, and we quickly switched on our second flashlight.

It was strange how completely our new goal had pushed aside our earlier fears. We had stopped worrying about what might be lurking in the ruins. The beings that had left supplies in the great circular chamber had clearly planned to return, yet we had entirely forgotten about them, as if they had never existed.

The figure in front of us was large—about six feet tall—but we knew at once that it wasn't one of them. They were much bigger and darker, and according to the carvings, they moved across land with a confident, fluid motion despite their ocean-adapted tentacles.

Still, the sight of the pale creature ahead of us filled us with a deep, primitive fear, sharper than anything we had felt before.

Then, just as quickly, the tension broke.

The white shape waddled clumsily into a side passage, answering the squawking calls of two others already waiting inside. It was only a penguin—though not like any we had ever seen before.

It was huge, larger than any known species of king penguin. Even stranger, it was completely white, an albino, with barely visible slits where its eyes should have been.

We followed it into the archway and shined both flashlights onto the trio of birds. They didn't react to our presence at all, standing motionless except for an occasional flap of their wings or an awkward shuffle of their feet.

They were all the same—giant, eyeless albino penguins of an unknown species.

Their enormous size reminded us of the ancient penguins carved into the walls of the Old Ones' city. It didn't take us long to conclude that these birds were descendants of that prehistoric species. They must have survived by retreating into a warm, underground world where complete darkness had erased their pigmentation and caused their eyes to wither away.

There was no question about where they had come from. Their home was the vast abyss we had been seeking.

The realization that life still thrived in the abyss filled us with a strange mixture of excitement and unease. The ancient sea below was still warm enough to support these creatures, which meant it was still habitable. The thought of what else might exist down there unsettled us deeply.

We also wondered why these three birds had wandered away from their usual home. The dead city above had clearly never been a nesting ground, and the fact that they were completely unbothered by us suggested that no other visitors had disturbed them recently.

Had the others—the beings who had passed through before us— done something to alarm them? Had they tried to hunt these penguins for food?

We doubted that the strange scent from the ruins—the one that had made the dogs panic—would have affected the birds in the same way. After all, their ancestors had once coexisted peacefully with the Old Ones. That bond must have lasted in the abyss for as long as the Old Ones had remained there.

A part of us regretted that we couldn't take photographs of these strange creatures. Despite everything, the scientist in us was still drawn to the discovery.

But we had no time to dwell on it. We left the penguins to their squawking and continued toward the abyss, now completely sure that it remained open.

The occasional tracks left by the birds showed us the exact direction we needed to go.

***

Soon after, we started moving down a steep corridor with a low ceiling. Unlike the other passageways, this one had no carvings at all. This made us hopeful that we were finally nearing the tunnel entrance. As we continued, we passed two more of the strange, pale penguins.

Then, the passage suddenly opened into a massive underground chamber that took our breath away. It was a perfect, upside-down dome—about a hundred feet wide and fifty feet high. Around most of its edges were low archways leading to other passages, but one section was different. There, a huge, black arched opening interrupted the smooth curve of the chamber, stretching nearly fifteen feet high. This was the entrance to the abyss.

The ceiling of the chamber was carved with fading designs meant to resemble an ancient view of the stars, though the work was rougher than in earlier sections. A few of the eyeless albino penguins wandered aimlessly around, indifferent to their surroundings.

The gaping tunnel sloped downward at a sharp angle, its opening decorated with strange, grotesque carvings. From within, we thought we felt a faint rush of warmer air and perhaps even saw a hint of mist rising. We couldn't help but wonder what else might exist down in the darkness—what kind of creatures, beyond these strange penguins, might still live in the endless tunnels and caves below the city and mountains.

We also thought back to Lake's early reports from the expedition. He had once suspected that a wisp of smoke had been rising from a distant mountain peak, and we had seen a strange haze near the rampart-like summits. Was it possible that these vapors were connected, rising from deep underground through cracks and channels from the Earth's core?

As we stepped into the tunnel, we saw that it was about fifteen feet wide and high. At first, its walls, floor, and arched ceiling were made of the same massive stone blocks as the city above. Some sections were decorated with worn, repetitive carvings in a crude, later style. Despite their age, both the stonework and the carvings were remarkably well-preserved.

The floor was mostly clear, aside from a light layer of dust and some tracks—penguins heading outward and something else moving inward. As we continued, we noticed the temperature rising steadily. Soon, we had to unbutton our heavy coats.

We wondered if there were actual volcanic heat sources below and whether the underground sea we sought might be warm.

Before long, the stone walls gave way to solid rock, though the tunnel kept its same precise, artificial shape. Some sections of the floor were so steep that grooves had been cut into the rock, possibly to help with footing.

Now and then, we passed side tunnels that weren't marked on our map. None of them seemed large enough to get lost in, but we made note of them. If we ran into anything dangerous ahead, these passages might offer a place to hide.

That eerie, unidentifiable scent that had followed us throughout the ruins was now much stronger.

It was probably reckless to continue under these conditions, but the urge to explore the unknown can be stronger than fear. After all, that same urge had brought us to this desolate part of the world in the first place.

We passed a few more of the huge, pale penguins and wondered how far we still had to go. The carvings had suggested a mile-long descent to the abyss, but we had already learned that their scale wasn't always reliable.

After about a quarter of a mile, the strange scent in the tunnel became overwhelming. We made sure to keep track of every side passage we passed. Unlike at the entrance, there was no visible mist here—likely because there was no cool air to create a contrast. The temperature kept rising, and before long, we came across something chillingly familiar.

Scattered on the ground was a pile of fabric—furs and tent cloth taken from Lake's camp. The way the material had been slashed into bizarre shapes made our skin crawl, but we didn't stop to examine it too closely.

Not long after, we noticed that the side tunnels were growing larger and more frequent. This suggested that we had reached the honeycombed caves beneath the foothills.

Then, a new and equally horrible smell filled the air. It was mixed with the original scent, but it was something different—something rotten. It made us think of decay, of dead things decomposing deep underground, or maybe of some strange kind of fungus growing in the darkness.

Before we could dwell on it, the tunnel suddenly expanded into a much larger space—something we had not expected based on the carvings.

The passage opened into an enormous natural-looking cavern, about seventy-five feet long and fifty feet wide. It had a level floor and multiple huge openings leading off into even deeper tunnels.

At first glance, this space seemed to be a natural cave, but when we shined our flashlights across it, we realized that wasn't entirely true.

The walls were rough, and the high ceiling was covered in stalactites, but the floor had been deliberately smoothed.

Even more unsettling was the fact that there was no dust, debris, or loose rock anywhere—not even in the large tunnels branching off from the chamber. Everything looked unnaturally clean.

The air here was thick with the strange new odor, so strong that it completely masked the other scent we had been following.

Something about this place felt wrong—more disturbing, in an unexplainable way, than anything we had encountered before.

The passage leading forward was clear, so we weren't in danger of getting lost among the many tunnels, but we decided that if things became more complicated, we would start marking our trail with paper again. Since the floors here were so strangely spotless, we couldn't count on leaving footprints behind.

Continuing forward, we shined our flashlights on the walls and froze.

The carvings had changed.

We had already noticed that the artwork in the tunnels was less detailed than the sculptures in the city above, showing signs of decline in skill. But now, something was different—not just in quality, but in style.

The carvings ahead of us were crude, rough, and completely lacking in detail. They had been cut much deeper into the rock than before, but their designs barely rose above the surface. It was as if something had erased the original artwork and then replaced it with new, sloppy carvings.

Danforth suggested that this was a second layer of engraving—a crude attempt to rework the designs after the original images had been worn away or destroyed. These new carvings followed the same basic mathematical patterns as the Old Ones' earlier work, but they were distorted, almost like a mockery of the old tradition rather than a continuation of it.

We didn't have time to study them in depth, so after a quick glance, we kept moving.

By now, we saw and heard fewer penguins, though we thought we could hear faint, distant cries from somewhere far below.

The awful new smell was nearly unbearable, but the original strange scent had almost completely faded.

Then, ahead of us, wisps of vapor rose in the air, confirming that we were nearing the great abyss. The rising heat told us that the sunless sea was close.

But then, unexpectedly, we saw something blocking our path.

It wasn't penguins.

We turned on our second flashlight, first making sure that whatever lay ahead wasn't moving.

Chapter XI

Once again, I found myself at a point where continuing forward became almost unbearable. By now, I should have been used to the horrors we had faced, but some things leave wounds too deep to heal. Some memories only make the terror feel fresh again, no matter how much time passes.

Up ahead, we saw something blocking the smooth floor, and at almost the same moment, an overpowering stench filled the air. The foul smell that had followed us through the tunnels was now mixed with something even worse—something that reeked of death and decay.

When we shined our second flashlight on the obstacles ahead, we immediately knew what they were. We only dared to move closer because we could already tell from a distance that these things were just as lifeless and powerless as the frozen bodies we had uncovered in the strange graves back at Lake's camp.

Like those earlier specimens, the forms ahead of us were incomplete—but in this case, the damage was much more recent. A dark green liquid oozed across the floor around them, pooling thickly in the dim light.

There were only four bodies, even though Lake's reports had suggested that at least eight of these creatures had been ahead of us. What had happened down here? What kind of battle had taken place in the dark?

We knew that penguins, when attacked, could fight back fiercely with their beaks. And somewhere in the distance, we could still hear the muffled cries of an entire rookery. Had these beings stumbled into a nesting ground and been attacked?

But as we looked at the bodies, that didn't seem likely. The damage was far too extreme—penguin beaks could never have caused this level of destruction. And the huge, blind birds we had seen earlier had seemed strangely calm, showing no signs of aggression.

Had there been a fight among these creatures themselves? Were the missing four responsible for what had happened? And if so, where were they now? Were they close? Could they be waiting for us?

Uneasy, we glanced at the smooth tunnels leading off from the main passage as we crept closer, reluctant to see the truth.

Whatever had happened, it had clearly scared the penguins enough to drive them from their usual home. The battle must have taken place near their distant nesting ground, deep in the abyss, since there was no sign that they normally lived in this part of the ruins.

Maybe there had been a desperate chase through the tunnels—one side trying to flee, the other in ruthless pursuit. It was easy to imagine the scene: nameless horrors clashing in the dark while swarms of terrified penguins scattered in every direction.

Slowly, cautiously, we approached the twisted remains. I wish to heaven we had turned back instead. I wish we had run as fast as we could from that cursed tunnel, with its unnervingly smooth floors and its strange, crude carvings that mocked the artwork of the past. I wish we had fled before we saw what we saw—before the sight burned itself into our minds forever, never letting us breathe easily again.

Both of our flashlights focused on the remains, revealing exactly what had been done to them. The bodies had been crushed, twisted, and torn apart—but the most horrifying detail was their heads.

Or rather, the fact that they had none.

All four bodies had been completely decapitated. Their strange, starfish-like heads were gone. And as we stepped closer, we saw that they hadn't been cleanly cut off, but ripped away. The injuries looked like they had been caused by some horrific suction or tearing force rather than any kind of blade.

The thick, dark-green fluid that leaked from their wounds filled the air with its sickening stench. But worse than that was the other smell, which was now stronger than ever. It was something completely unfamiliar, something that made our skin crawl.

Only when we were nearly on top of the scene did we see where that second, more awful odor was coming from.

And in that moment, Danforth let out a terrible, broken scream—one that echoed wildly through the ancient passage, making the air itself seem filled with madness.

I nearly screamed as well, because I knew exactly what had flashed through his mind.

I had seen the same carvings he had.

I had stared in horror at those ancient murals, which told of an unspeakable war that had taken place over a hundred and fifty million years ago—carvings that showed the horrifying fate of the Old Ones when they were betrayed by the very creatures they had created as servants.

Those murals had been disturbing enough when they were only stories from the distant past. But now we had come face to face with something that should have never been real.

The scene before us matched those nightmare images exactly.

The bodies were covered in a thick, glistening black slime.

It clung to them, still wet and fresh, reflecting our flashlight beams with an unnatural iridescent sheen.

We saw more of it smeared across the newly carved walls—in a series of grouped dots that suggested something even worse than the corpses themselves.

In that moment, we understood true terror.

And it wasn't because of the four missing creatures. We weren't afraid that they would attack us.

We knew—we knew—that they were already dead.

Because they had come home.

After untold ages, they had finally returned to their ancient city. And in doing so, they had walked straight into the fate that had once destroyed their kind.

These beings were not evil.

They had been explorers, returning to the only home they had ever known.

And in the end, nature had played the cruelest joke imaginable.

Just as in the past, long before humans ever walked the Earth, something had been waiting for them.

Something had never left.

And now, as we stared at the remains in front of us, we realized with horror that we were not alone.

They had not even been savages—so what had they really done wrong? They had woken up in a strange, frozen world, in a time they couldn't understand. Maybe the barking, fur-covered creatures had attacked them first, and they had fought back in confusion, defending themselves against both the dogs and the strange, pale beings wrapped in unfamiliar clothing.

Poor Lake. Poor Gedney. And poor Old Ones.

They had been scientists until the very end—just like us. What had they done that we wouldn't have done in their place?

Their intelligence and determination were incredible. They had faced the impossible, just as their ancestors had long ago. They had studied and adapted, surviving through ages of unimaginable change. No matter what they were—radiates, plants, monsters, creatures from the stars—they had been people.

They had crossed the frozen mountains where they had once worshiped and lived among ancient tree ferns. They had returned to their city, now abandoned and cursed, and read its history carved into the walls—just as we had. They had tried to reach others of their kind, the ones who still lived in the deep, dark places they had never seen.

And what had they found?

These thoughts raced through Danforth's and my mind at the same time as we stood frozen, staring at the headless, slime-covered remains. Our eyes shifted to the sickening, distorted carvings on the walls—those mocking, twisted versions of the past—and then to the fresh, glistening dots of slime smeared beside them.

And we understood.

We knew what had survived down there in the massive, sunken city beneath the black abyss.

At that very moment, a pale mist began to rise from the tunnel, curling toward us as if responding to Danforth's panicked scream.

The realization of what we were seeing—the headless bodies, the unnatural slime, the horror that had been waiting in the depths—paralyzed us. For what felt like an eternity, we stood there like statues, unable to move or speak.

Later, when Danforth and I talked about that moment, we realized we had both thought the exact same thing.

In reality, only ten or fifteen seconds had passed.

But that mist, swirling toward us, seemed to be pushed forward by something else—something massive, something unseen.

Then, suddenly, a sound shattered our thoughts.

It made us question everything we had just decided. And it broke the spell of terror that had held us still.

Without hesitation, we turned and ran.

We sprinted blindly, faster than we thought possible, past the startled, squawking penguins, retracing our path through the tunnels of the ruined city. We raced through ancient corridors sunken in ice, through the vast circular chamber, and up the endless spiral ramp.

Our minds were empty of everything except one desperate, overpowering need.

We had to reach the open air. We had to escape. We had to see daylight again.

***

Then we heard it—a terrible sound—that made us run wildly toward the fresh air outside, desperate to escape.

***

One more thing shook everything we thought we understood: the sound we heard matched what poor Lake had described during his dissection—the sound we thought could only come from the beings we had just decided were dead. Later, Danforth told me it sounded exactly like what he had heard faintly back at that corner above the glacier. It reminded both of us of the eerie wind-like sounds we'd heard near the high mountain caves.

I know it might sound childish, but I have to mention something else because of how strongly Danforth and I both reacted. We'd read the same books, and we were both thinking of that strange story Arthur Gordon Pym by Edgar Allan Poe. In it, a mysterious word is shouted over and over by huge, ghostly white birds in the far south: "Tekeli-li! Tekeli-li!" That's exactly what the strange sound seemed like—soft, musical piping over a wide range of tones, carried by the white mist behind us.

We didn't wait to hear more. The moment the first few notes came through, we took off running. We knew how fast the Old Ones were, and if even one of them had survived the massacre, it could easily catch us. Still, we hoped that maybe, if it caught us, it wouldn't hurt us—maybe it would be curious, especially if we didn't act threatening. After all, if it had nothing to fear from us, maybe it wouldn't want to harm us.

We knew hiding was useless, so we used our flashlight to look back while we ran. The mist behind us was starting to thin. Maybe we were about to see one of them alive for the first time. Then came the sound again—"Tekeli-li! Tekeli-li!" And when we realized we were actually gaining distance from whatever was chasing us, we started to think maybe it was injured. But we couldn't take any chances. It was clearly heading toward us because of Danforth's scream. The timing was too perfect to ignore.

We had no idea where the other, even more terrifying creature—the huge, disgusting thing that Lake had only guessed at—might be. It was a shapeless mass of slime that had once ruled the deep and pushed into the hills. We didn't know if it was still alive, and it hurt to think that we might be leaving a wounded Old One behind to face such a monster alone.

But thank goodness we didn't stop. The mist got thicker and started swirling faster. The penguins we'd passed before were now panicking—squawking, screaming, and acting far more frightened than they had earlier. The piping sound came again—"Tekeli-li! Tekeli-li!" That's when we knew we had been wrong. The thing wasn't hurt. It had just paused when it saw the bodies of its kind and the disturbing slime writing on the wall above them. We would never know what that message said, but the way they buried their dead showed us how much they cared.

Soon our flashlight showed the opening to a large cave where many paths came together. We were relieved to be leaving behind the disturbing walls that felt eerie even when we could barely see them. We had a new idea—maybe we could lose the creature in the maze of tunnels ahead. Several of the blind white penguins were in the cave too, and their fear of the thing chasing us was extreme.

We decided to dim our flashlight to its lowest setting and keep it pointed only forward. Maybe the noise from the scared penguins would cover the sound of our footsteps. Maybe they would confuse the thing and send it the wrong way.

The fog was swirling thickly all around us. The tunnel floors ahead looked different from the rest—messier, less shiny—and we hoped that even the creature's strange senses wouldn't be able to tell which way we went. We worried that we might get lost too, but we knew we had to keep going straight toward the dead city. If we got lost in the maze of foothill tunnels, we'd be done for.

We made it out, so we must have picked the right tunnel while the creature took a wrong turn. The penguins alone wouldn't have saved us, but together with the thick mist, they helped us escape. We were lucky the fog stayed dense just long enough—though it started thinning right before we left the tunnel.

That's when we saw it—just for a second. The mist cleared enough for us to catch one awful, blurry glimpse of the thing chasing us. It happened just as we turned for one last, desperate look before turning off the light and blending in with the penguins. If fate had been kind to hide us, it was cruel to show us even that much—because that single glimpse is the reason half the terror still haunts us to this day.

***

We probably looked back because of some deep instinct—like when something is chasing you, and you just have to see what it is. Maybe it was just a natural reaction to a question our bodies picked up without us thinking about it.

Even though we were focused only on escaping, not paying attention to anything else, some part of our brains still noticed something strange. Later, we figured it out. As we ran from the slimy remains of those headless shapes and the thing chasing us got closer, we expected the awful smells to change. Logically, the bad smell from the creatures should have faded, and the one from our pursuer should have taken over.

But that didn't happen. Instead, the newer and even worse stench stayed strong—and it was getting sharper and harder to ignore with every second.

That's when we looked back—both of us at the same time, though maybe one of us started and the other copied. We pointed our flashlights straight into the thinner mist, maybe just out of fear, or maybe hoping to blind whatever it was before we shut the lights off and ran again through the maze of penguins.

It was a terrible mistake. Like the old stories of people who paid dearly for looking back—like Orpheus or Lot's wife. And then that awful, eerie sound came again: "Tekeli-li! Tekeli-li!"

Danforth lost it completely. The next thing I remember was him chanting like he'd gone mad—saying something that would have sounded like nonsense to anyone else. His shaky voice echoed off the walls, mixing with the penguins' cries, bouncing around ahead of us— and thankfully, also behind us. He hadn't started chanting right away, or we might not have made it. I don't want to think about what might've happened if he'd reacted just a little differently.

"South Station Under—Washington Under—Park Street Under— Kendall—Central—Harvard—" He was naming subway stops from back home in Boston, as if clinging to something familiar. But to me, it didn't feel comforting. It felt terrifying—because I understood what horrible thing had made him think of that.

When we looked back, we thought we'd see something terrible chasing us—something we already imagined. But what we saw wasn't what we expected. It was far worse. It looked like something out of a nightmare—a monster that should never exist. The best way I can describe it is like standing on the tracks and seeing a huge subway train rushing toward you from deep underground, with strange lights shining from it. But we weren't on a platform. We were on the tracks, and it was coming straight at us.

It wasn't a train, though. It was a massive, slimy, shapeless thing. It glowed faintly, with bubbling lumps that kept changing shape. Dozens of glowing green eyes appeared and disappeared all over its surface as it slid forward, crushing penguins and gliding across the slick ground it had cleared.

That chilling, mocking cry kept ringing out—"Tekeli-li! Tekeli-li!" That's when it hit us—we finally remembered what the Shoggoths really were. They were creatures created by the Old Ones, formed and controlled completely by their makers. They didn't have voices of their own. The only sounds they could make were ones they had learned by imitating the voices of those ancient beings who were no longer around.

Chapter XII

Danforth and I remember coming out into the large, carved dome and retracing our steps through the massive halls and passageways of the dead city. But these memories feel like pieces of a dream—we don't recall choosing to move, how we got through it, or even how tired we were.

Something about leaving that ancient place felt strangely fitting. As we climbed the sixty-foot stone shaft, gasping for air, we passed rows of carvings showing brave scenes made by the Old Ones, still untouched by time. It felt like a goodbye from them, left behind fifty million years ago.

When we finally pulled ourselves out at the top, we stood on a pile of broken stone blocks. To the west, curved walls of taller ruins loomed, and to the east, the jagged peaks of huge mountains rose above crumbling buildings. The sky above was swirling with thin, icy clouds, and the cold felt like it reached deep inside us.

Within fifteen minutes, we'd found the steep slope leading to the lower hills—the same ancient ledge we had used before. Ahead, we spotted our large plane parked among scattered ruins, sitting dark against the slope.

Halfway up the hill, we stopped to catch our breath. We turned around for one last look at the strange, twisted shapes of the city behind us, now silhouetted in the mysterious light of the western sky. The early fog was gone, and the shifting ice clouds had floated straight above us. Their strange shapes looked like they were about to form a pattern—but held back, as if afraid to fully appear.

Behind the weird city, far out on the white horizon, we saw a faint, ghostly line of violet mountains. Their sharp peaks reached into the sky like needles, glowing against the pink light of the west. The high, ancient plateau sloped up toward them, with the dry path of an old river snaking across it like a shadow.

For a moment, we stood in awe at the strange beauty of the scene. But then, slowly, a feeling of dread took over. Those far-off purple mountains could only be the cursed range we had heard of—the tallest on Earth, and full of dark secrets. Legends said they held things too terrible to name, and were feared by even those who once ruled the world. Nothing from Earth had ever walked there. Only strange lightning visited them, flashing across the polar skies.

If the ancient carvings in the city were true, those mountains were nearly three hundred miles away. Still, they stood out clearly, their jagged tops like the edge of some alien world about to rise over the horizon.

Staring at them, I couldn't help but think of the old carvings showing what the river might have carried down from those cursed slopes. I wondered if the fear the Old Ones had felt was real—or just superstition. They had been careful with their warnings, barely showing the true horror.

I remembered that the northern part of those mountains came close to the coast near Queen Mary Land, where Sir Douglas Mawson's team was probably exploring—less than a thousand miles from us. I hoped nothing would lead them past the protective coastal mountains. Just thinking this way showed how shaken I was—and Danforth seemed even more rattled.

Still, before we even reached our plane, our fear shifted to the smaller, but still massive, mountain range we had to cross again.

From where we stood, the dark, broken slopes rose sharply to the east. They reminded us of the strange, dreamlike paintings of Nicholas Roerich. We thought about the tunnels hidden inside, and the shapeless creatures that might still crawl through them—even reaching the highest points. The idea of flying near those cliff openings again made us panic. The wind howled through those caves, sounding like eerie, twisted music.

Worse still, we noticed patches of mist near some of the peaks—just like what poor Lake must have seen when he mistakenly thought there were volcanoes. We couldn't help but think of the thick, cursed mist we had just escaped—and the dark, terrifying pit it came from.

***

The plane was still in good shape, and we struggled to pull on our thick flying gear. Danforth got the engine running without any problems, and soon we were taking off smoothly, rising above the terrifying city below us.

High above, the sky looked strange and unsettled. The clouds of icy dust were swirling in wild, unusual patterns, showing that the upper atmosphere was unstable. But at the altitude we needed—around 24,000 feet—the flight went smoothly enough.

As we got closer to the sharp mountain peaks, we heard that strange, eerie whistling sound again. I noticed Danforth's hands shaking as he tried to steer. Even though I wasn't an expert pilot, I started to feel like I might handle the crossing better than him. I motioned to switch seats, and he didn't argue.

I focused hard, trying to stay calm as I looked ahead at the narrow gap between the mountains, where the sky beyond glowed a reddish color.

But Danforth, now freed from flying and deeply stressed, couldn't stay still. I could feel him shifting and twisting in his seat, glancing back at the city behind us, then ahead at the strange, hollow mountains with their cave mouths, then to the snowy hills, and finally up at the twisted clouds above.

It was then—right when I needed to stay focused the most—that Danforth suddenly screamed. His wild cry shook me so badly that I lost control of the plane for a moment. Luckily, I pulled myself together just in time, and we made it through the pass safely. But I'm afraid Danforth was never the same after that.

He wouldn't tell me what final horror made him lose control like that. I'm sure it's the main reason he later had a breakdown. As we flew back toward camp, we shouted a few things to each other over the engine noise and the wind, but it was mostly reminders of our promise to keep everything a secret.

All Danforth ever said about what he saw was that it wasn't something inside the mountains we crossed. It wasn't the caves or the cube-covered cliffs. He said it was something like a mirage—something he saw up in the sky, behind the distant violet mountains that the Old Ones had feared so deeply.

Sometimes, when he's not fully himself, he mutters strange, scattered phrases. He talks about "the black pit," "the carved edge," "proto-Shoggoths," "five-dimensional shapes with no windows," "the original jelly," "eyes in the dark," "the color out of space," "Yog-Sothoth," and other weird ideas. But when he's thinking clearly, he says it was just his imagination—probably influenced by all the creepy things he used to read.

Danforth is one of the few people who's ever dared to read the full version of the Necronomicon, locked away in our college library. It's full of dark, strange stories that could haunt anyone's mind.

As we flew over the mountain range, the upper sky was definitely filled with swirling vapor and clouds. I didn't see directly above us, but I can guess how those spinning clouds could have formed strange shapes. The way light can reflect and bend in those high layers might have made it look like something was really there. Maybe his mind filled in the rest—especially after everything we had been through.

But in that moment, the only thing Danforth kept shouting—over and over—was that one terrifying, echoing word: "Tekeli-li! Tekeli-li!"

THE END

Thank You for Reading

Dear Reader,

We hope this timeless classic has sparked your imagination and enriched your literary journey. Now that you've turned the final page, we want to share a vision for the future of reading—one where every classic you've ever wanted to explore is at your fingertips, in a format that best suits your life.

We'd like to invite you to gain immediate, unlimited digital & audiobook access to hundreds of the most treasured literary classics ever written—along with the option to secure deluxe paperback, hardcover & box set editions at printing cost. Together, we can spark a new global literary renaissance alongside our small, independent publishing house called "The Library of Alexandria."

Thousands of years ago, the Library of Alexandria stood as a beacon of knowledge—until it was lost to history. We aim to reignite that spirit of preservation and discovery right now, in the modern age—only this time, it's accessible to all, in every language and every format.

Picture a world where every timeless classic, novel, poem, or philosophical treatise is not only available to read but also updated for today's readers—modernized, translated into any language or dialect, and ready to enjoy in any format you choose, whether that is in an eBook, audiobook, paperback, or deluxe hardcover & box set version a printing cost.

By joining our movement to rebuild the modern Library of Alexandria, you become part of an unprecedented mission to offer:

- **Unlimited Audiobook & eBook Access to the Greatest Classics of All Time**

  Instantly explore thousands of legendary works, from Plato and Shakespeare to Jane Austen and Leo Tolstoy. All are instantly ready to read or listen to, giving you a complete literary universe at your fingertips.

- **Paperback & Deluxe Editions at Printing Costs:**

  Purchase any title in a paperback, deluxe hardbound, or deluxe boxset edition at printing costs, shipped right to your doorstep. Curate your personal library of Alexandria with editions worthy of display—crafted to last, designed to captivate, and delivered straight to your door.

- **Modern translations for Contemporary Readers in all languages and dialects**

  Discover a vast selection of classics reimagined in clear, current language—no more struggling with outdated phrases or obscure references. Next to the original versions, we aim to offer translations in as many languages and dialects as possible.

  As we continue our translation efforts and add new languages, readers everywhere can connect with these works as if they were written today. By bridging linguistic divides, you're contributing to ensuring that these timeless stories become more meaningful, accessible, and inspiring for people across the globe.

- **Your Personal Library of Alexandria:**

  Over the months and years, you'll curate a unique physical archive of classics—each volume a testament to your taste, curiosity, and love of knowledge. It's not just about owning books—it's about curating a cultural legacy you'll cherish and pass down for generations to come.

- **Join a Global Literary Renaissance:**

  Your support fuels an ongoing mission: allowing us to reinvest in offering deluxe print editions (including special boxsets) at their true cost, broaden the range of available formats and translations, and extend the reach of these works to new audiences worldwide. By joining today, you're not just preserving a legacy of masterpieces; you set in motion a powerful wave of literary accessibility.

  We are more than a publisher—we're a movement, and we can't do it alone. Your support lets us scale our mission, preserving and reimagining history's greatest works for tomorrow's readers.

Become a Torchbearer of knowledge.

Thank you for picking up this book and allowing us into your literary journey. As you turn the pages, know that you're part of something larger: a global effort to keep these stories alive, share their wisdom across borders and generations, and spark a true cultural revival for the modern era.

If this resonates with you—please consider taking the next step by visiting:

www.libraryofalexandria.com

With gratitude and a shared love of knowledge,

The Modern Library of Alexandria Team

Visit:

www.libraryofalexandria.com

Or scan the code below: